The
Magellan House

Also by John Rolfe Gardiner

Double Stitch

In the Heart of the Whole World

Great Dream from Heaven

Unknown Soldiers

Going On Like This

The Incubator Ballroom

Somewhere in France

The Magellan House

Stories

John Rolfe Gardiner

Illustrations by Joan Gardiner

COUNTERPOINT
NEW YORK, N.Y.

To Joan

Previously published stories in this work appeared in the following:
Ontario Review; "The Doll House," 2004; "The Ricus Adams" (as "The Endless Shelf") 2002
American Short Fiction; "Morse Operator," 1992; "The Magellan House," 1993
Southwest Review; "Fugitive Color," 2003
The New Yorker; "The Voyage Out," 1994

Published by Counterpoint
A Member of the Perseus Books Group

Books published by Counterpoint are available at special discounts for bulk purchases in the United States by corporations, institutions, and other organizations. For more information, please contact the Special Markets Department at the Perseus Books Group, 11 Cambridge Center, Cambridge MA 02142, or call (617) 252–5298, (800) 255–1514 or e-mail special.markets@perseusbooks.com.

Designed by Reggie Thompson

Library of Congress Cataloging-in-Publication Data

Gardiner, John Rolfe.
   The Magellan House stories / by John Rolfe Gardiner.
      p. cm.
   ISBN 1-58243-233-3
   1. United States—Social life and customs—Fiction.   I. Title.
PS3557.A7113M34 2004
813'.54—dc22
                                                              2004004932

04 05 06 / 10 9 8 7 6 5 4 3 2 1

Contents

Rasson-Pier performed the first of
his handstands on the ship's railing.

1

The Voyage Out

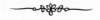

Tony Hoskins, at twelve, was an intellectual child, wary of sensation. Not a prodigy exactly, but at the head of his form at Cacketts School. He could declaim on several tales from Chaucer, and on the paths of the planets, even on the curious journeys of human sperm and ovum, although he hadn't a clue about finding a girlfriend or what might be asked of him in pleasing one.

On this day he was saying all the wrong things, first to his father. "Daddy, at least I'll be sailing on a British ship, under a British flag."

"Actually not," he was told. "It's an American vessel. You'll be all right."

This was before the German began to aim his torpedoes at Yanks, before his subs began to hunt in wolf packs.

"Not to worry," his father went on. "You'll be in convoy."

Why a convoy, if no need to worry? His father, in Royal Army lieutenant's uniform, bare of medals, could not answer.

Hoping to put his religion in order before embarkation, Tony looked to his mother. "Tell me again, what's the Trinity?" he said unexpectedly just before the ship pulled out.

"Tiresome boy," she said. "Three in one and one in three. If you don't understand that, you shan't have a chocolate."

Again he was confused; his mother's simplistic formulation seemed at odds with her piety. Hardly off the gangplank, his legs rubbery with fear, he didn't want candy, only assurance that this huge and blunt-prowed merchant ship with a woman's name, the *Ellen Reilly*, riding high in the water, would come to safe port across the Atlantic and that his new school would be tolerable.

He saw other parents retreating, crying into handkerchiefs, stumbling off the boat and along the dock, giving their boys up to the sea and a new world. The drawn lips of his father and mother began to quaver as they turned away. And enemies appeared beside him, his second-form mates Booth and Jeffries, full of questions.

"Do the lifeboats have engines?"

"Is it daytime in Canada?"

"Will we take a secret course to avoid submarines?"

The same boys who despised him in the classroom, who had called him "twit" and "wonkie" for his privileged conversations with the masters, were hovering around him. Why should he nurse their fears?

And here came Rasson-Pier, who was older, a fifth-former who had once caned Tony for impudence. Rasson-Pier told them all to shut up. He said the lot of them should be ashamed for leaving their country in wartime. And if it were up to him, he'd be in uniform, not in retreat.

"Hoskins, you're in my cabin," he announced. "See that the beds are made taut."

Rasson-Pier, tall, well muscled, and lording it over the others from Cacketts, with gray eyes under blond bangs, and sufficient beard to be permitted a razor in his kit.

Riding down the channel from Folkstone, Tony tried to use his father's advice—*Think of the ship as the floating island of a country still at peace*. Over on their left was France, which he knew to be alive with Germans; on the right, his own island, which, after dark, would be under attack again from the air.

Only three weeks earlier Tony's headmaster, strolling across his playing fields at night, had been killed by a bomb far off its city target. A miraculous and devastating event, a direct hit on school morale. In the ensuing rearrangements of the school year Tony and six other boys, and Mr. Pardue, history master of the stunned academy, had been booked on this empty supply ship—refugees for resettlement in a Canadian boarding school.

The *Ellen Reilly* came clear of the coast and swung to the west. There was no convoy, only open sea. Tony took the blank journal his father had given him that morning (with the suggestion, five hundred words a day at bedtime) and threw it over the side.

"You mustn't be angry," Pardue admonished. "It will only be fourteen days." But Tony gestured at the zigzag wake of the ship, the pattern of fear they were leaving on the sea behind them.

"Never mind," Pardue told him, "you'll be at their organ in two weeks. Maybe some of your Chopin, eh?"

"Maybe some of his Chopin, eh?" The other boys played with the line, but anxiety cracked their voices.

In the boys' new school, an oddity of brick and stone nestled in farm fields to the west of Toronto, they came to be known as "The Boys from Cacketts" or "The Boys from Cacketts Minus One," after the tragedy at sea, while their teacher shepherd became "Pastor Pardue" among his new colleagues, who found him to be a total loss as an instructor, and a fount of useless homily: "There are no ifs in history."

They were set apart as a curious subculture among the relatively coarse population of Canadian boys—a little band with a higher order of fealty to the King, and led in intellect by the youngest, the pale scholar Tony. He was allowed in to the school chapel each afternoon to practice at the organ, while the others were led off to a field to fight over a leather ball or flail away with cricket bats. Tony had come with two copies of his medical excuse, proof of his asthma—one to be filed in the school infirmary, and the other for his pocket. Thus reprieved from athletic torment, he was free to demonstrate his case that the body's only sensible purpose is to carry around the brain.

On October 28, 1941, Lieutenant Gerald Hoskins dashed off a note, from his office in the London Cage, to his son, Tony, at the Charter Bridge School.

Dearest Tony,

Horrible, horrible. We had the awful news before your letter arrived. There are not enough tears in the world to answer for the loss of a child. And such a well-favored boy by all reports. You must be numb. Our only response to such an untimely death can be surpassing love for those who survive. Try to think of our love for you.

You say the Trinity was revealed to you on the crossing. Very well, but remember you are stuck to the planet by gravity, and from an Oriental perspective you may be upside down, worshiping the devil. But no more—the colonel is calling.

P.S. No, we don't keep animals here. Nor are there Nazis in dank cells. "London Cage" is simply the informal name given to this interrogation center. From time to time I will write you from my office here, where I won't have your mother looking over my shoulder. The address here must remain unknown to you. Your letters should be posted home.

A second letter from the lieutenant to his son, dated November 15, 1941.

Dearest Tony,

Nothing from you this month. Our assumption must be that you have settled in and found a schedule suited to your special needs. We have a report from Dean Hastie, who tells us your academic proficiency is "not balanced by contribution to community."

While offering the excuse of your harrowing journey, he cites you for sarcastic remarks about the Canadian students, for shirking work in the school garden, and resisting dress regulations.

Though your mother and I agree that shorts are not suited to the climate, the answer is to bundle heavily on top. Wear the sweater, scarf, and cap as prescribed in the school manual. You know that long trousers come in the third form, just as they do at Cacketts.

You may have heard on the wireless that we are managing quite well in the air. When I am not translating or writing interrogation reports, they have me reading prisoners' mail. There, I've told you a little secret, and you must keep it to yourself.

A sympathy committee has been got up here. We take turns visiting the Rasson-Piers. When you have a moment you will write them whatever you can muster of David's last days. Perhaps something you found heroic in him, or you could express your wonder at his potential. As the last to see him you are a target of their curiosity. They have questions beyond the police type, which they are too discreet or grief-bound to ask. It will be your job, now or later, to anticipate and console.

It's too awful to think he might have been showing off acrobatically so close to the side. Showing off for whom? one asks, since no one saw him go overboard. So dreadful for all of you, wondering if he were hiding somewhere or actually lost at sea.

We hope the investigation has ended and we pray for your happiness. Or, I should say, your mother prays and I beg of fate. Have you been faithful to your journal? It will be a revelation to you in time to come.

After the blank journal had gone over the side, Mr. Pardue had gone to his cabin to fetch a substitute, another bound notebook with marbled cover.

"Your father told me how much this means to him," he said to Tony. "I've put in some starter lines for you." He pointed to the first page.

> *For every trouble under the sun,*
> *There be a remedy or there be none.*
> *If there be one, try and find it,*
> *If there be none, never mind it.*

"You take it from there," he said, smiling.

Before they left the channel someone had puked. And now the boys' stomachs felt the rise, fall, and side shift of the Atlantic's heavy quartering waters. The first officer promised only more discomfort. "That's right— we're empty," he announced on the boat deck. "And the higher she rides, the further she rolls."

He had come from the bridge to lay down ship's rules for the Cacketts boys. At mealtime they would go to the mess deck, officers' side. The rest of the day they would remain in their cabins doing schoolwork. For exercise they could walk the main deck, but only with Mr. Pardue's supervision. The bridge and hold of the ship were off-limits. The boys must stay out of the crew's cabins and out of the galley, or risk losing a hand to the steward's cleaver.

The officer had no sooner turned back when Rasson-Pier performed the first of his handstands on the ship's railing. Upside down, he had winked at Tony as the ship rocked in a rising swell.

"See that, Hoskins?" The older boy's hand was on Tony's shoulder as they went to their cabin. "You can count on me, you see. I'll be watching out for you. You have nothing to fear from the chaps in Canada."

Dean Hastie at the Charter Bridge School to the parents of Tony Hoskins in Brasted, Kent, November 30, 1942.

We normally write to parents of the boys from Cacketts at the end of each term. However, the head and I felt it would be wrong to delay in reporting that Tony is in a fair way to surpassing school records for third-form boys in Mathematics, Latin, and History of the Empire. He might achieve similar distinction in Composition if he could be kept to assigned topics.

We should recommend your son for immediate advancement to fourth form if his social and emotional maturity were up to the same marks. As you know, at Charter Bridge we strive to develop the fully rounded boy. We had expected that in his second year here Tony would have put new-boy diffidence behind him and joined with a will in some extracurricular pursuit.

Perhaps Tony has mentioned the motto cut in stone over our chapel door. "Remember Now Thy Creator in the Days of Thy Youth." We take the charge seriously, so you must not misunderstand when I say the religious conversion your son experienced on his journey here is troubling in its intensity. Our chaplain cannot shake him from his testimony that the Trinity was revealed to him on the ocean as three glowing balls. We see no joy in his faith.

I must tell you that the transfer has not been a complete success. The boys from Cacketts tend to remain a clique, though they sometimes quarrel among themselves. Your son does not seem to be a member, even of this separate band. We sense a residual grieving here for the loss of their young idol, and a weight of unfinished business. One boy has suggested that Tony's original account of the events at sea may not be reliable. And now, more than a year after the fact, our Mr. Pardue comes forward to say that your son may have kept a journal which might clear him of all suspicion. We wouldn't think of invading his privacy without warrant. Perhaps you would advise him to open relevant pages to our scrutiny.

A brighter note. Our music instructor is leaving Charter Bridge this month, and we are asking Tony to fill in as chapel organist for Sunday service and Wednesday vespers. It's our little scheme to get him more involved.

On the journal's first page Pardue's verse has been scribbled over and splashed with ink.

Sept. 23, 1941. Aboard the *Ellen Reilly*: The ship is black, red, and rusty. Sailed 1420 Greenwich. R.-P.'s stunt behind Pardue's back takes everyone's breath. Supper: mashed potatoes, bright-yellow gravy of uncommon viscosity, and salty fish, white and cooked to a mush like the potatoes. One serving of greens a day; we missed them by coming aboard too late for lunch.

Tonight Jeffries came into our cabin crying. He wanted to know why I was put with R.-P. R.-P. said wouldn't the Germans love to see him like that. Jeffries left snivelling. R.-P. asked me down from my upper to play cards on his bunk. Twenty-one. No money, playing for favors, he said. I lost terribly, what do I owe him? R.-P. has torch with extra dry cells. He will allow me to use it to keep my notes. Says he's at sea in Latin. Quite so! And I, a second-former, might help.

Booth came in shaking with fear. The idiot thinks he heard a torpedo propeller passing under us. No one can sleep.

A year after the crossing, the notebook was more useful to Tony as a chronology of odd particulars than as a thoroughgoing journal—a skeleton on which his memory hung the dangerous flesh, the things he would never have written down. For example, the way Rasson-Pier's tone had changed after lights-out, from cold command to simpering—as if he were taking the part of a woman in a play.

With the notion of water rushing in to drown him in his sleep, Tony had sneaked out of his cabin in the middle of the first night and wandered through dim-lit passages, down metal stairways, into empty cargo compartments. Somewhere close to the throbbing center of the ship he heard a horse whinny and a lion roar. Alarmed by what he took to be his own inventions, he became confused in retreat, and spent an unconscionable time finding his cabin again.

From Lieutenant Gerald Hoskins at the London Cage to Tony Hoskins at the Charter Bridge School, April 13, 1943.

Yes, we support your refusal to show any part of the journal. Violation of your private thoughts is tantamount to rape of the spirit.

There is mischief here, too. I'm sorry to say we are no longer speaking with the Rasson-Piers since they find more comfort in the gossip of the Jeffrieses, passed along by their son Arthur. A poisonous little chap, I'd guess, but you would know better than I.

Yes, traits in an individual can be correlated with national origin, the pieties of Mr. Pardue to the contrary notwithstanding. It's quite possible that the impulsive and vainglorious side of David Rasson-Pier was passed along by the father's French parents. As to the question of cultural distinction, consider the opening lines of two letters which crossed my desk this week, the first from a German: "Dear Mother, The most awful thing has happened. We have been captured by the English and are being held in Oran, waiting transfer to a prison camp in America."

The second from an Italian: "Dear Mama, The most wonderful thing has happened. We have been captured by the English and will soon be on our way to the United States."

Don't mistake me. I'm not advocating one attitude over the other. But if your Pardue doubts the relevance of my example, I suggest he visit the prison camp in Bowmanville. I'm told the Germans there are goose-stepped by their officers to the mess hall, where Italians happily prepare the food and banter about the women waiting for them in the town.

No, we do not hold it against the dean for denying you further use of the chapel organ. Really! A two-octave glissando at the end of "God Save the King" while the school waited for amen! Did you expect to get away with that?

Guard your journal.

September 25, 1941, aboard the *Ellen Reilly*.

This whole ship trembles with the thump of its engines. Diesels, I'm told. Above this constant drumming is the daylong rattle of electric paint chippers as the crew works at their endless chore of scraping and painting. They'll go from bow to stern, then start all over again.

No one actually studied today. In spite of the din, fell asleep over my books. R.-P. woke me before Pardue came in. Anyone caught napping during study time gets twenty-four-hour cabin confinement. I've been made tutor of second- and third-formers. Pardue says those not prone to seasickness must minister to those who are. He is. So is Jeffries. I am not.

Booth apologized for rudeness. As R.-P. has taken my part, others are shifting colors, too, seeking my favor. At present, most of them are unable to function. While they moan in their bunks, I explore.

Dolphins weaving under the prow. Watching them for most of an hour before slipping below again. One of the crew stopped me. Only wanted to talk. This was Sam, an able-bodied seaman, who is missing two fingers, and limps. Asked did I know there were unfortunates below. Heard animals again in lower cargo compartments. Couldn't find them.

Night walk. The deck was dark but for moonlight. No outside lights permitted. Passageways only faintly lit. Memorized numbers on doors and did not get lost. No one believes I saw a black-haired girl in bathing costume. She was rattling a cup of coins and chanting something sad, as if practicing to be a beggar. Someone called from another compartment,

"Raklo! Raklo!" and she stood still as a stone. If R.-P. doesn't believe any of this, why does he keep asking how old the girl was and what she looked like? Very young. Her skin a mottled ochre.

Someone filched my breakfast orange. R.-P. boxed Booth's ear. Doesn't matter who did it, he says, just doesn't want it happening again.

Tony had put aside pen and notebook when Rasson-Pier offered his soft invitation.

"Do you want to come down to my bunk?" All the courage and bluster vanishing again.

"No."

"For a little visit?"

"No."

"You're to be kind to those who aren't feeling well."

He didn't believe the older boy was sick, only dodging the books for another day, with the sympathy of Pardue.

"No."

From Dean Hastie at the Charter Bridge School to the parents of Tony Hoskins in Brasted, Kent, May 21, 1943.

Looking toward vacation, we are suggesting that Tony not remain in dormitory with Mr. Pardue and the other boys from Cacketts. We would not want a repeat of last summer's incident. With your permission, Tony will spend the interim at the Croyston farm, which provides the school with milk and eggs.

A picture of the family is enclosed. In truth, I think the Croystons would welcome an appropriately innocent companion for their shy daughter, Margaret, and your son seems well suited for the job. Though the family won't provide intellectual stimulation, they keep a wholesome life, devout yet not without humor.

Tony will be expected to help with farm chores, perhaps just the thing for the continuing melancholy. A break from the high academic standard to which he holds himself, and from his difficult religion. May I quote him? "The faith at Charter Bridge is to true faith as water is to wine." Perhaps the justification for his little musical joke on the school.

We have not discounted homesickness—the long, unnatural separation from the two of you. Too, the Rasson-Pier case will not go away. As I explained months ago, the initial investigation produced little but tears and mystery. Should we discourage the family from persisting? So many loose ends. From their distance can they be sure the appropriate questions were asked? Our Cacketts boys have kept the stew at a boil.

You ask again for the facts free of the children's fantasy. The ship's log reported the child missing on October 1, 1941.

Captain Andrew Shad made inquiries and established that David had been given to reckless displays of daring. He concluded one of these must have been the boy's final act.

The *Ellen Reilly* made its first port, Halifax, on October 7. Our boys disembarked and were detained there two days for questioning, first by the R.C.M.P., later by a visiting magistrate from London. Before the investigation was completed and the captain's finding upheld, the ship had already taken on grain and tinned food, and sailed the night of October 8 for Baltimore. There the loading of war supplies was completed. With the same officers and crew the boat turned back for England on October 14.

We now believe there was another element on board the *Ellen Reilly* between England and North America, a group kept apart from legitimate ship's company but sighted several times if we are to believe the Jeffries boy and your own child. A band of Polish performers? Gypsies? Lithuanian Jews? How they came to be on the ship and where they disembarked are as open to speculation as their nationality.

We had, too, the crass report of a seaman named Sam, put off the boat in Halifax for the theft of a pair of shoes. He was a rough sort who befriended several of the Cacketts boys and entertained them with bawdy talk in his quarters, which they knew were off-limits.

This Sam testified to having seen passengers in the hold. He fouled his account with details of a dark young lady, little more than a child by his word, offering her favors to several of the crew. If people didn't believe him, he said, they could ask our boys what she'd do.

As to the mysterious travelers, whether Captain Shad gave them passage as a humanitarian gesture or for his own profit is unclear. Their arrival was not recorded by Canadian immigration. Shad, who survives as a master in the merchant marine (the *Ellen Reilly* went down in January, off the Azores), does not deny that such a group could have been stowaways during his command.

We are told that the docks in Halifax are too closely patrolled for any such band to have disembarked without papers. They may never have come ashore in North America, unless they were spirited off the ship in Baltimore. The United States was not yet at war, and security was doubtless lax. This seems a remote possibility but so does their very existence on board. Given the curious tatterdemalion migrations and urgencies of wartime, their passage is not beyond belief. Perhaps sympathy, reinforced by coin, eased the path into America.

Again we ask you to urge your child to come forward with his journal, if it exists, and any relevant information that might soothe the family. We have again advised the Rasson-Piers against a crossing.

Though we find Tony a difficult boy, the faculty is interested by him, and, if I may say so, fond of him. We would see nothing unnatural in an infatuation he may have had for David Rasson-Pier. These things are common as hiccups among schoolboys, and are left behind as naturally as they arrive.

Our comptroller reminds me that we have not received your share of reparations for the water damage in Tony's room last August. We appreciate your faith in Tony's innocent part. However, a clear culprit was not found, and all the boys from Cacketts must share the cost of repair.

September 26, 1941, aboard the *Ellen Reilly*.

Ocean calm but Sam says we're headed into "weather to pump the boys' stomachs again." Complimented me for my sea legs. Told him R.-P. is faking it to avoid the books. If he were sick, how could he use the ship's rail for a gymnast's horse? He spins his legs right around over the side. Jeffries, Phillips, and Booth have all seen him do it. Gives me the willies. Booth said he wouldn't care if R.-P. lost his balance.

Found another route to the forward cargo bay. Hid in a crate and watched the show. Bales of hay set out in a circle. There appears to be a family circus traveling with us. Preparing its act for America? A small black bear was brought in, muzzled and growling softly. Is this the noise I took for a lion's roar?

Can bears survive on ship's rations? There is also a miniature pony that whinnies like a full-grown horse.

I suppose the man must throw knives every day or get out of practice. Tonight the girl was pitiable, with her chin fallen to her chest, and her arms stretched wide, like Christ on the cross, and surrounded by the steel blades delivered in rapid order. By her father? Her brother?

A woman unleashed the bear and placed it on the seat of a small bicycle. Maybe upset by the motion of the ship, it could not keep the pedals going and tumbled over.

R.-P. says I must pay my gambling debt. I'm sure he cheated me.

Tony had recorded nothing of what happened the next day, or the following night when, after lights-out, Rasson-Pier had climbed into the upper bunk with him, whispering urgently, "the others needn't know."

He wrote nothing of his haunted sleep, of this famous athlete poking around behind him with his stupidly swollen thing.

From Captain Gerald Hoskins at the London Cage to Tony Hoskins at the Charter Bridge School, September 20, 1943.

Dearest Tony,

Your mother and I would transfer you to another school in an instant if it were reasonably within our power. Our distance, our ignorance of alternatives, and the dean's reluctance to recommend "some inferior academy" all work against us. It is an outrage that your notebook was stolen. We have demanded an apology from Hastie. He seems to us a great blandifier. Believe me, you have nothing to fear from him but his dangerous good will.

It is out of the question for you to return to England now. The Americans have only just begun to appreciate the logic of convoys. In the meantime their coastal waters have become a continent-long fireworks display, with U-boats sinking tankers and supply ships at will. Hardly a time to play "Red Rover, Red Rover, Let Tony Come Over."

There is nothing to be ashamed of in your account of the crossing save the occasional grammatical lapse, though eyebrows are raised at the mention of gambling. The hounds have what they've bayed for, a dry bone. Now let them bury it.

The Dean says you worked admirably for the Croystons and amazed their church youth fellowship with the force of your testimony. I know your mother's letters are full of admiration for your spiritual awakening. She warns me not to disrupt your faith with petty sophistry. Still, I can't approve a dogma which condemns to perdition all those beyond its pale. This is *entre nous*.

It's no special boast to tell you I've been promoted to Captain. All officers here at the Cage have taken one step up. So, nothing heroic, though I am credited with devising a new purgative for the tight-lipped Germans. I stamp their papers N.R. (*Nach Russland*, to Russia) and their mouths run a torrent.

From Dean Hastie at the Charter Bridge School to the parents of Tony Hoskins in Brasted, Kent, January 24, 1944.

Again the school offers its full apology to you and your son. That Tony's journal should have been taken from his room is altogether unacceptable. That pages were copied and distributed is despicable.

We don't know who stole the notebook. It appeared in the office of our school paper, the *Charter Sentinel*, where the editor, one of our senior boys, cut a stencil of certain pages and ran them off on the mimeograph machine. This misguided chap, who comes to us from Detroit with a warped notion of press freedom, has been relieved of all journalistic duty.

I now believe it was a mistake to badger Tony for his record of the voyage. The notes have only raised the anxiety of the Rasson-Piers, who insist they could not be the work of a twelve year old. In their new anguish they suspect the cruel mischief of an adult—a postdated fabrication supporting the police report of a foolhardy, self-inflicted death.

The family's theory was reinforced by your son's admission that the notebook was not the original, lost at sea, but a substitute provided by Mr. Pardue. Thus, he too is a subject of suspicion. The evidence of a missing page, the ragged edge in the journal, where a sheet was torn from it, adds to our confusion. The more so, since this was apparently part of the entry for October 2, 1941, the day after David's disappearance was first recorded.

We have assured the family that the original notes are in Tony's skilled hand, and that your son is capable of the vocabulary and sentiment, even the occasional poetic flourish. We couldn't swear to the dating of the entries, but have no reason to doubt their honesty. The headmaster and I were disturbed by references to gambling, punishable at Charter Bridge by immediate expulsion. However, we accept Tony's word that nothing of value was to be exchanged, only favors.

That the mysterious travelers belowdecks are transformed into a Gypsy circus seems a wild leap of imagination. Our school physician advises me that the mind under stress (all the Cacketts boys have ac-

knowledged their numbing terror of submarines)
may take refuge in illusion.

A copy of the mimeographed notes is now in the
hands of the police, who have asked to speak with
Tony once more. Be assured that the school's attorney
will again be on hand to prevent investigative bullying. If Tony chooses to tell them he remembers nothing, that will suffice. We pray for a return to academic
tranquillity.

September 28, 1941, aboard the *Ellen Reilly*.

The rattle of the paint chippers stopped for a
merciful hour this morning. Pardue took advantage of
the relative quiet, calling a meeting in his cabin to
rally spirits. He never rose from his bunk. The air was
horrid.

Our workbooks will be collected tomorrow,
though there is not a word or cipher in most of them.
Took Pardue some tea this morning and was caught
out by Phillips watching from the door of his room.
Phillips says it will all come out when we reach
Canada, all the broken rules. And there will be
whippings. Told him there is no corporal punishment
at Charter Bridge. He seemed much relieved. He
asked what R.-P. talks about and does he do stunts in
the cabin.

Pardue whined pitifully for me to take his tray
away. The smell of toast and margarine was making

him ill again. Jeffries tried to trip me at his doorway. Called me "suck-bottom."

I can tolerate the pitch and roll of the ship. Also, the further one descends through the lower decks, the less one notices the roll. Sam says the people below are stealing food. The galley is missing a dozen tins of beef. Bear provender? Captain Shad is furious and says we've been roving through his ship against orders. I'm the one. I suppose the others would rather die in their cabins.

I have seen a periscope like a black needle in the waves behind us.

October 1, 1941, aboard the *Ellen Reilly*.

R.-P. did not return to the cabin last night. A search for him began this morning. Certain we won't find him.

There followed a line obliterated, washed over with ink. How many times had he been asked, "If you wrote 'certain,' were you not certain?" and "Why did you cross this out?" Why should he tell them, "I did not cry with the rest"?

On the evening of September 29, Rasson-Pier followed Tony down through the maze of passages to the performance chamber, complaining repeatedly of the grease stains the metal stairways were leaving on his trousers.

"Periscope? Girl in a bathing costume? What next, Hoskins?"

"Why didn't Pardue put Phillips with you?" Tony asked him. "Someone more your age."

"I asked for you," he said. "Thought it might give you a boost."

The hero of the Cacketts playing fields had asked for him? Anxious about displeasing Rasson-Pier again, he prayed the girl would be there.

She was sitting on a bale, with her back to them. A long black dress appliquéd with red and orange rings gave the effect of contouring her ample young figure in tight-fitting bracelets.

"Run along," Rasson-Pier ordered. "I'll speak to her alone."

"She doesn't speak English," Tony said. "I could try a little French for you."

Why had he wanted to be helpful? He was only pushed aside.

The girl turned and stared at them without modesty. Before Rasson-Pier could sit beside her, she had risen, taken his arm, and was leading him away through the hatch at the far end of the compartment. Perhaps a fortune-teller, Tony thought, leading him to a private place to read his palm.

From Dean Hastie at the Charter Bridge School to the parents of Tony Hoskins, Brasted, Kent, January 26, 1944.

I dare to presume a friendship has developed between us in our pursuit of your son's welfare. This letter following close on the heels of the last is prompted by a surprising turn in the Rasson-Pier case. There is now a theory the boy may be alive.

We are told by the police that there was a family row before the voyage, a shouting match in which David called his parents such names as "pale cowards" and "funny little people." He threatened never to come back if they packed him off to Canada. This was followed by one of his acrobatic demonstrations, a walk on his hands down a stone stairway in front of their home in Kent. Certainly a thoughtless display in front of his troubled parents.

The imaginations of the Rasson-Piers must be racing along with the flow of news and rumor from the families of our Cacketts contingent. I'm told that "Gypsy circus" is oxymoronic, that, while Gypsy children are often sent out to beg, the families never perform or work for money, unless it be in telling the future.

The Rasson-Piers now cling to the frail chance that a rebellious David might have been drawn to, or charmed away by, this band that must have intended to land in America. That they may have seen profit in his gymnastic virtuosity. But who is to say they were Gypsies? Haven't they also been called Lithuanian Jews and Polish performers?

I turn again to Tony's situation. Why do the other children continue to torment him? If the authorities don't trust his written account, how will they credit his oral testimony?

Your child has taken refuge in his faith. All worthy counsel, he avers, comes from the three-person God, though we know he looks daily to his letter box for guidance from you. Your son has lost weight. We try to see that he eats well.

From Captain Gerald Hoskins at the London Cage to Tony Hoskins at the Charter Bridge School, February 15, 1944.

Dearest Tony,

We're proud of you. Stick to your guns, and ask yourself this: Why would they have you impeach yourself? What good could come of it? Can the lost boy be brought back? If you find yourself in a compromising box, don't jump out in public. If there is something to say that can cause only humiliation, take it to this higher being of yours, all three of him if necessary. I am dead serious. Take proper nourishment, and hold on. You will cross this way in victory the moment the Atlantic is secure.

Early on September 30, Rasson-Pier had come back to the cabin quite exhausted.

"They don't wash, you know," he said. He sighed and fell asleep. Tony covered for him through the morning, calling "Studying, please" when the others knocked for their morning chats.

At noon, Rasson-Pier was awake and irritable.

"Who doesn't wash?" Tony asked him.

But the older boy was looking into the future. "If you say anything of what's happened in this cabin, I'll report your funny business when I caned you at Cacketts."

"What business?"

"The way you enjoyed it. Even more without trousers."

"I never. Whatever do you mean?"

"Yes, well, who will they believe?" He fell back on his bunk. "Perhaps I'll tell them anyway," he said.

He slept again for several hours, woke, and asked, "What if she's given me the disease?"

"What disease?"

"You sap. The one that takes your brain."

"I believe there's a cure for that."

The older boy nodded slowly.

"Don't look for me tonight" was the last Tony heard him say.

If the girl's odor displeased him, if he thought her infected, why had he gone to see her again? Goatish, Tony had heard his mother say, but would not a goat demand exclusively a mate of opposite gender?

The October 1 journal entry had concluded, "The ship went a drunken path through the glowing sea when the sky was torn into three ragged black sheets by lightning."

Tony had stayed out on the open deck that evening in order to avoid his roommate. Standing at the stern, he watched the serpentine course of the ship recorded in the roiled wake. With the first bolt of lightning, he swung around and saw a figure far up the deck, balanced upside down and turning with his hands on the rail, his legs, at that instant, over the side. And someone was standing there, close to him, perhaps the girl. All went black and a moment later they were all brilliantly lit by a second bolt. The spinning body was disconnected from the rail, floating out into the night.

So obvious of Rasson-Pier. Showing off for the girl. Performance was the only language they had in common. Tony made his way forward in the dark, but the two of them had vanished. No time to applaud the trick; the next act of his floating circus had already begun. A spectral ball was gliding down the stay that ran from antenna mast to the bow. It split into two glowing spheres, and then there were three of them, evenly spaced, moving back and forth along the taut metal line. He watched for several minutes until they merged into one again and disappeared.

October 2, 1941, aboard the *Ellen Reilly*.

Is he pestering the dolphins? Sawn into rude portions by sharks? Have I seen the spirit of God in triplicate?

The next page had been torn from the notebook.

From Tony Hoskins at the Croyston farm to his parents in Brasted, Kent, August 23, 1944.

The summer has flown. I am two inches taller. Six feet! The second haying is finished. I was allowed to work the rake, an old-fashioned thing once pulled by a horse, this season by an ancient tractor, petrol being available. For two weeks I've been sitting on the metal seat of the rake and lifting its tines at each windrow with a hand lever. As a result my right arm is appreciably muscled, and I must do something to bring the left into balance.

Yesterday a man came to replace some rotten boards in the north end of the haymow. I was asked my estimate of the barn's height at the point of the gable. I could tell them quite precisely, I said, by measuring the shadow of the barn and that of a pole of known length, then applying simple geometry. By the time I gave my answer, Mr. Croyston had made a calculation of his own and the carpenter was on his way to the lumber yard. My figure was off by half a foot, Mr. Croyston's correct to the inch. So my fancy education is a thing of some amusement here, though Margaret is keen to share my books and ideas.

Last Thursday I was asked to escort her to a "young people's" in the village. It's not the social gathering it sounds. There is some flirtation, but only so much as is possible when you are seated in church pews under the eyes of a preacher.

Between hymns, each boy and girl is expected to rise, in turn, and share a faith-affirming experience. I think I blushed awfully when the minister's eyes fell on me, but I was able to stand and tell again of the three balls of fire over the deck of the *Ellen Reilly*. By the end of my story the pastor's eyes were brimful, and *I* was embarrassed for *him*. Margaret, seated to my right, took my hand when I sat down again.

From Captain Hoskins at the London Cage to Tony Hoskins at the Charter Bridge School, September 10, 1944.

A note to tell you that civilians are crossing again! Given proper escort, it appears to be safe. I've made inquiries, and will find a berth for you the moment space is available on a secure ship. You've been so long there under brutish circumstances. It would be cruel of us to leave you longer than is prudent for your safety. We know that there is still talk of your journal's missing page. I fear the gossips will never give it up.

From Tony Hoskins at the Charter Bridge School to his parents in Brasted, Kent, October 5, 1944.

Please do not book passage for me. I'm content and intend to finish here.

Fair questions have been raised, and there is something I want to clear up about the voyage out. When I saw David Rasson-Pier spinning above the ship's rail, I thought he'd learned a new trick. It never occurred to me he was out of control. Not until it was far too late to give an alarm.

The following day I returned to the same place on the deck. Looking down, I saw a row of three lifeboats suspended over the side. One could speculate about David's having fallen onto the canopy covering one of these and climbing back onto the deck below. But the chance is so minuscule. Believe me, he perished at sea. It's too late to raise another slim hope that can only give anguish.

If you must know, the page torn from my journal held my thoughts on the family belowdecks. Particularly the girl, and Rasson-Pier's use of her. I did not invent the girl. Think of her under a rain of knives, and try to imagine throwing knives at me for a living.

The dean is quite mistaken about Gypsies. They frequently take itinerant work, and are known for their rapport with animals, notably as trainers of circus acts. And when I went down in the ship, I heard *"Raklo! Raklo!"* called out like a crow's warning. It's the Gypsy word for a non-Gypsy boy. I doubt I will see her again, or know what befell her, but we were all Gypsies on that voyage, I now believe, and I would cry *"Raklo!"* now to those who did not make the crossing. Our chaplain says the war has blown seed, good and bad, to all points of the compass, and it remains to be seen what will germinate. High hopes for me. But what of the rootless Gypsies? I like to think of the girl and her family moving across America, performing, escaping, from one camp to the next.

I'm confident her troupe survives. Almost as certain as I am that David Rasson-Pier is dead. The passage of time has not weakened my resolve not to write to his family. You will have to guess at my reasons.

About my "hard faith," as Hastie calls it. You shouldn't think I ever believed the fireballs over the ship's deck were the actual embodiment of the Trinity. I took them, rather, as a phenomenal sign of Mother's faith. No more periscopes after that. They helped me complete the crossing without going mad. And why should that sign be erased now, by some scientific explanation? Really, for men who profess faith, some of my instructors are quite hopelessly literal.

For all that, I like the teachers here quite as well as the masters at Cacketts. The Atlantic may, as you say, be secured for Allied shipping. Nevertheless, I don't wish to return to England before graduating from Charter Bridge.

From Dean Hastie at the Charter Bridge School to the parents of Tony Hoskins in Brasted, Kent, November 20, 1944.

We shall never hope to understand this war's random terror, why we are spared here in our snug academy while refugees from all walks are driven pillar to post. I do believe we can now take hope in these few boys from Cacketts who were washed up on our shores. I am their dean, yet I sense that they are children no more. The heat of war has fired them, and they shine with a new hardness and brilliance. Especially your son.

You would not recognize Tony. His second summer on the Croyston farm did wonders. He is quite filled out in athletic proportion, and happy as we have never seen him. It will please you to hear, too, that your son has found common ground with students and masters alike, and can be seen on occasion roughhousing and joking with his mates from Cacketts.

Something has cleared the air. There is less ostentation in his religious assertion. I don't think the other boys ever believed he was guilty of any complicity in the Rasson-Pier tragedy. Rather, they resented his claim to a private audience with God on the voyage out. Without boasting, we give our faculty credit here, in particular our Department of Physical

Science. Mr. Theonel believes his lecture on electricity was responsible. As he says, "Knowledge must rush in where dispelled superstition leaves a vacuum." Tony now concedes that the three balls of light he saw on the ship's antenna must have been static electricity, the phenomenon called "St. Elmo's fire."

We think it gave him comfort to learn from our history instructor that early mariners also believed they witnessed holy bodies in the rigging of their ships—the *corpus sancti*, or corposants, as they called them. Tony will be returning to you with a new maturity. Once more, he has our permission to practice his music on the chapel organ. Eventually, I'm sure, he'll be trusted to play for our services again.

The third anniversary of David Rasson-Pier's disappearance will not have escaped your notice. It was observed here by a special prayer at evening vespers, and a reading of this note from the family: "We believe our son perished at sea by his own dangerous devices. To those children who survive, we offer our blessing. Your useful lives must be our monument to David's memory." The school is much relieved by their sad but sensible resignation.

The Charter Bridge students filing in to the final chapel service of the year were surprised to see Tony Hoskins seated at the organ. Excited, they squirmed and whispered in their pews, as if assured of a sacrilege to spice the imminent summer rebellion.

They were disappointed to hear scarcely a hint of the expected irreverence. Buttercup's theme floated over "Faith of Our Fathers," so cleverly hidden in tempo and contrapuntal disguise that no one but the new music instructor was wise to it. From the choir he winked approval at his richly gifted student.

Melanie coaxed her work
toward art with an irritating
two-note plainsong.

2

Fugitive Color

Spring

"Duck. Watch your head."

Reynolds was nudging Devorah from behind, preventing her retreat. To pass under the ancient town wall she had to go to her hands and knees, and crawl through the opening.

"The monks did it for hundreds of years," the director explained. "When they arrived as initiates they had to demonstrate their humility. I did it when I first came here, and I like my students and faculty to start the same way."

Devorah remembered him from their first meeting in New York as a vain, white-maned little man, aggressively persuasive, though nothing quite like this. Inside the walls, she stood up covered with orange dust, fine as talcum, more humiliated than humbled. She was being watched by a small group of students standing in the narrow street above her.

"Hallo," a young man called. The girl holding his hand flipped her hair and snickered as Devorah tried to tidy herself. Without waiting for an introduction the students turned their backs and retreated up the cobbled passage in a noisy herd.

"A lot of spunk in this bunch," Reynolds said. He had made his own entrance through the proper gate, and was trying without success to brush the new color from Devorah's clothes.

"It's another lesson we take from our tours in Roussâtre. Here the landscape can paint us. We heard you way down there." He was pointing a mile away. "Winding up the switchback."

The whine of her car had been the signal for them all to come down and see if she'd submit to Justin's rite of arrival. He was going on about the hole in the wall, a passage opened to allow goats free range hundreds of years ago when medieval sieges had given way to a wary commerce between the hilltop citadels.

"I'll tell you all about the monastery later. One can imagine . . . "

When they told her in Apt, "You can't miss Roussâtre," they didn't mean it was a tourist's obligation. They meant it was visually inescapable. Of all the perched villages in the Vaucluse it was the only one standing out against the cerulean heavens like a red-earth fresco. The rest were gray and inconspicuous, most of them capped with the ruins of ancient châteaux. This one was built of the same limestone, but painted with the ocher mined from its own cliffs, and was topped with what Reynolds called "the Monastery of the Brothers of the Little Gate," now home to his art school.

Devorah had come here to teach painting her way—tools before talent, and a step-by-step isolation of the issues that painters must recognize and master if they cared about an honest translation of the visual world to canvas. She'd been enticed by the region's art history, and by the school's slick brochure, *The Palette of Provence*. Professional instruction, it said, for fifty students. Classes *en pleine air* on terraces overlooking the Luberon Valley. Savory meals by a chef from Arles served on rustic oak tables in the monastery's cool refectory. Cheeses, baguettes, *vin du pays*.

Founder and director Reynolds, whose abstracted Gallic portraits were held in profitable favor at a Manhattan gallery, had been convincing, too, at her winter interview, talking her into a commitment to three sessions in his painter's heaven. He promised her idyllic private quarters with a balcony giving on the valley that had provoked van Gogh's color riots.

"A neat package of artistic energy with classical rigor. Just what we've been looking for. A wonderful hire." Reynolds' description of her in the staff newsletter reached her en route at American Express in Paris. It made her sound like a shelved commodity available for any art school's consumption. As she read, she felt the chip on her shoulder growing heavier:

"Devorah Francke comes to us from her studio in Baltimore, Camden Loft, where she has taught for twelve years. Her work, in a figurative tradition, will speak for itself."

And so would she, Devorah promised herself, approaching Roussâtre in her well-worn VW Super Beetle. The car, considered a gas guzzler anywhere east of Calais, she'd acquired from her American friends in Avignon, a couple she'd traded with for three small landscapes of the Pyrenees. Through a clever transfer of title and plates she was avoiding a killing sales tax, and gaining six months of licensed grace.

These Avignon friends wondered at her choice of schools. At thirty-five wasn't she too mature, too settled, for their sort of experiment? Why wasn't she going to the better-known, more respected art school in LaCoste, only twenty kilometers from the Roussâtre academy?

What did they mean?

To be fair, they said, the bunch in Roussâtre had only been at it for a few years. All the bad news that had come their way could be behind them. The reports of the director's cultish practices were probably exaggerated. After all, how could one man have undue influence over students cycling in and out, season by season? With Devorah's wheels, her passable French, and habit of independence, they said, she'd be a match for whatever situation she found there. It wasn't as if she were signing on as a credulous scullery maid in de Sade's château. She couldn't be kept against her will. No, looking so pert and fetching, her black hair clipped short, looking so French actually, she'd be more a target of provincial swain and their suspicious mothers than of the Americans around her.

Making an exaggerated fuss over her three rapidly painted landscapes—she could tell they didn't really like them—her friends sent Devorah on her way to the Luberon, though not before revealing their certain knowledge of a suicide at the Roussâtre school two years earlier. That and a recent report in the Arles paper about a week of intestinal horror, which had forced the director to replace his chef with a man more sure of his mushrooms.

After so much foreshadowing, Devorah's arrival, her passing under the yoke of tradition, suggested more tedium than menace. It came home to her as a bit of a shock that she had signed on for three whole seasons of the director's loopy enthusiasm—and students, at first glance, of swollen self-esteem, wary of any who might classify them according to their abilities rather than their individuality. If they were looking for easy credits to carry back to their universities, they'd misread her résumé.

The little monastery was magnificent, as advertised. From her balcony Devorah looked down on a feudal geometry of green and brown, a pattern of ancient cultivations, now given here and there to early wheat. There was a trapezoid of asparagus, a narrow rectangle of melon vines, a square of garlic. On the lower slopes were orchards in bud, and on the opposite hillside, grape vines following to the horizon in disciplined ranks.

The floors and walls of her rooms were cozied with rugs and woven hangings of wool dyed with the Roussâtre ocher. There was a rope bed, an armoire carved with *fleur de lis* in the center, fox and crow on side panels, and a line of verse—*tenez en son bec un fromage*—which she was able to translate as "holds a cheese in his beak," but was not able to identify. Beside the armoire were provincial chairs and bureau—all glowing warmly in the golden light of mirrored candle sconces that someone had lit, though the room might have been brighter if they had pulled open the curtains to the sun still available through the balcony's glass doors. And miracle of the sacred stone-walls-turned-secular, pipes ran through them—plumbing.

On the oak shelf just over the bed was a single book, a biography of the Marquis de Sade. She heard a toilet flush, and a young woman, plump and comely, walked in.

"You've come at last," she said, extending a hand theatrically.

"We share the same bathroom. Sandela Marks, I teach drawing. In case you didn't know it, you scored the prize quarters. I think they want to make sure you like it here. Justin's wife, Madame Pelagie, makes the room assignments. No one argues with her. I mean how could you argue with all that aggressive silence?"

Garrulous, Devorah thought, and prematurely friendly, already giving advice. "The worst thing you can do here is take yourself too seriously. Let the students do that. A bunch of spoiled brats, to tell you the truth. You know, artists by default, the banks and the advertising agencies wouldn't have them, and now they're here, pampered into overconfident artists."

Instead of leaving her alone to settle in, the woman sat coyly on the bed while Devorah used the bathroom. When she came out, she went rattling on about things Devorah would rather have discovered for herself. The attitude of the locals—aloof but tolerant—the food, a pretension that actually originated in cans; morale, best in the evenings, in the off-duty hours; and the weather, just like everywhere else, glorious and horrid, season by season, or day by day, "and it's true, the wind can drive you nuts."

She explained that Devorah's rooms were the only ones with double entry, triple if you included the bathroom between their quarters. Her bedroom opened into the upper hallway, and from her little study there was a narrow spiral stairway leading down to the old hall of worship. Sandela led her down the turning steps into the big chamber of ancient wooden pews, the school's main meeting room and lecture hall. The altar, partitioned with folding screens, served as administrative sanctum for Madame Pelagie.

"She's the mother superior," Sandela confided, "the ruling intelligence. She gives a dour balance to Justin's right-brain fancies. Go ahead, say hello."

Devorah stepped behind the screens for a quick "Enchantée, Madame Pelagie."

"And pleased to meet you, too."

But the woman wasn't pleased at all. Her dark hair was skinned back to a bun, revealing three small round scars, evenly placed on her high forehead. She kept right on with her work, head down, letting Devorah stand there until there was nothing to do but walk out.

As she took Devorah in tow to supper in the refectory, Sandela begged to be forgiven.

"I never thought you'd believe that was her real name. Pelagie is only what we call her behind her back. Her real name is Solange. But don't worry too much. She's heard it before."

Two French teens, Roger and Molan, hurried to serve the meal, too harassed to be polite. The students had all arrived and were seated at three long tables. They made a cocky gathering. One would have thought they were all acquainted, careless in their manners, already taking each other for granted, and searching over one another's shoulders, lest they lose out in the early skirmishing for romantic partners.

Reynolds, at the head of the first table, stood to welcome everyone.

"You're here," he told them, "to shed inhibition, to resist classification, to discover your own line and idiom. Each of you can make yourself a school of one. You should become the selves you've never met."

The gush made Devorah cringe. It was so at odds with the regimen he'd asked her to provide and that she'd promised him she would—submission of the ego to classic truths.

In her first class Devorah began at the beginning. She always did, no matter who the students, because most knew next to nothing about the materials they used. "Lapis lazuli, so expensive, was always saved for the Virgin's robe. Every pigment has its history. Some are fugitive and fade from the canvas with age. Others last for centuries. As painters it's your job to know the difference."

They were meeting in the monastery's central courtyard, under the open mouths of four gargoyles and Melanie Thayer, a thrust-lipped malcontent from Indiana.

"Are you telling us what colors to use?"

"Yes," she said, "I am. I suggest you start with a palette of six—cadmium yellow and red, alizarin crimson, ultramarine blue, cerulean blue, and raw umber. Plus white."

She led them through a color-matching exercise.

"Close isn't good enough. Close means you're not there yet."

She wanted them to experience the little rush that comes when the edge of the palette knife disappears against a background color. They must prove to themselves that from the discrete six they could reach any shade in the spectrum; they had access to all of it.

"Mix until you get it. It takes patience."

"Aren't we beyond this?" Melanie asked. She was circling her easel in frustration, declaring the assignment silly.

"You aren't," Devorah told her. "You're nowhere near it."

Seven of her ten painting students were enrolled in art departments at American universities, two had finished high school and were taking a year abroad before college, and one was a French walk-on, Celine, the wife of a melon grower from Cavaillon, whose bubbly mischief—"ooooh, how it comes from the tube!"—leavened the class discussion.

The two fresh from high school, classmates from West Point, Mississippi, Daisy and Janelia, were immediately won over to Devorah's step-by-step teaching method. Most of the older ones were trying to be good sports about it. It was all too clear they'd been encouraged in the sovereignty of self-expression and that comforting myth of their trampled genius.

These young people were not city rats. Most were orphans of suburbia. There wasn't a swarthy face among them. They dressed in tee shirts, torn vests, and pants that ballooned like pajamas, with here and there a beret on the more daring of them. Their pockets were not full, but there was money from somewhere; tuition for a single session was five thousand. It seemed odd they were continually bumming change and French cigarettes from one another.

She heard one of them say, "my head's been in sort of a Marxist place."

It was fortunate these philosophical plagues departed as easily as they arrived.

Arranging a still life of a goat skull and two giant figs in a terra cotta bowl, Devorah lectured against the tyranny of perimeter. Bulk, she told them, was best suggested by planes of color. It could not be outlined, only built from within. She enjoyed this. As a teacher she was sure of herself and encouraging to all, even the provocative Melanie, who was always ready with a subversive aside, and stage whispered to Celine at the easel beside her.

"Doesn't she know we define objects by the space around them? *If* we're so fixed on objects."

In the second week Devorah led them onto the terrace to simplify a landscape—sky to foreground—into four horizontal bands. Each silhouette to be a beautiful line.

"If the values and intensities are right," she told them, "then you can sense the atmosphere, the temperature, even the time of day."

"Another reductive lesson?" Melanie said she was fed up with reductive lessons.

Devorah promised her more of them. She'd never had a student quite like Melanie, who actually glared at her. It seemed to Devorah that the academy was full of people who didn't really belong there, didn't like each other or what they were expected to put up with. Her colleague Sandela was neither accomplished nor inspiring as a drawing teacher, though the students were responsive to her and her easy acceptance of their work. Her line was awkward, her drawings spoiled throughout with meaningless interruption that she must have thought artful but to Devorah suggested a small motor deficit. Sandela was pressing a regular evening companionship in the village bar-tabac, where she liked to sit and tell provocative stories about the director and his wife, drawing Devorah into a conspiracy against her will.

Of all the instructors Sandela was the old hand, the one who dared to make fun of Justin's monastery history. All bogus, she said. In the third week he had given his motivational lecture on Father D'Eclanton, the most notorious of Roussâtre's monks. According to Reynolds, he was not the *frère de libertinage* his countrymen accused him of being, but a misunderstood truth teller. All his paintings were burned after *Naked Jesus*, unveiled for the Easter Mass in 1781, was condemned by Rome and the crown. All that was left of his reputation was an acolyte's admiring commentary in a book of days, a spirited defense of D'Eclanton's *Joseph and Mary Unashamed.* "Which speaks to us as flesh to flesh," Reynolds explained.

Unavailable for viewing, this and the other paintings lived on as heroic lost work in Justin's imagination alone. He had stopped referring to "the painting Fathers" after a professor from Aix issued a statement that the monks of Roussâtre had actually been known for glassblowing and the construction of looms. No one had challenged the director's allusions to the Brothers of the Little Gate, though Sandela presumed this, too, was fiction.

One evening Devorah asked her the obvious question. "Why do you keep coming back?"

"One wants to do something for them," she said. "Really, they're only children. They haven't got a clue. And Justin is full as the Christmas goose. It's a game of gullibility he plays with them."

"With me, too?"

"I'd say so, yes. So far, anyway. What are you going to do about it?"

She let Devorah brood on that for a moment. "You know I'm right, don't you? Most of his students are tragic cases, failures in everything else. They've been taken in and pampered by art departments everywhere. They're over here, putting a little French patina on the résumés that have never been written, and probably never will be."

She could only answer "yes, you're right," though she was not comfortable saying so. Sandela seemed to be reading her mind, stealing her own assessments of Reynolds and his academy, reaching to touch her and staring intently into her eyes.

"Stick with me," Sandela said. "I'll show you how to handle him."

Devorah had no desire to stick with her. The thing was, she had no one else to talk to, and she let herself be drawn into this conspiracy of criticism, sometimes letting her silences be taken for agreement. And Sandela worked hard at bringing Devorah's doubts into the open.

First of all, the students weren't the least interested in working from life. Figurative studies were the drudgery they endured to get to their real work, the oils they troweled to the canvas and muddied with number fifteen brushes. Sometimes Devorah wondered why the village would tolerate all this—the presumption of talent behind the easels that cluttered their little terraces by day and American vomit on their cobblestones after the midnight closing of the bar.

On the hillsides peach trees burst into blossom and the fields below went into color shift. In the valley a dark brown stripe followed behind a plow and the clever Janelia alerted the class. "Look! A tractor pulling a paintbrush." And Janelia's pal Daisy produced a beginner's gem, a patchwork landscape that caught the scene with innocence. There was no mannered shaping, just an observant ordering of intensities that answered the clarity of the spring day.

"Don't touch it!" she told Daisy, who, unaware she was finished, was loading her brush for improvements.

Reynolds, who had dropped in on the morning lesson, seemed very pleased, too, affirming "a beginner's miracle." Actually he was there for a private word with Devorah. Taking her aside, he told her, "You might have guessed by now, Sandela can be a bit of a troublemaker. She set you up for your gaffe with Solange. That wasn't just an accident."

Devorah knew by then, from her sampling of the de Sade biography, that Pelagie was the name of the Marquis' wife and helpmate in his debaucheries, until she turned against him.

"It's just a little joke she likes to play on us. If she didn't pull in five or ten students each year, we wouldn't tolerate her. I'm sure you're aware she has only fair drafting skills. She's sort of a fixture here. A leaky faucet you could say, and a constant trickle of pessimism."

Devorah was about to defend her, but Reynolds raised his hand.

"Listen, you're doing beautifully. Just don't let Sandela get you into trouble." The way Sandela and the director complained of each other, one might have thought they were married; a steady carping, yet no dangerous ultimatums—as if, for better and worse, they were bound to each other.

Back in front of her class, he took another moment to tell them the story of Father D'Eclanton at the dry village well and his installation of a little sculpture of a boy making water. This was said to have produced the miraculous recovery of the spring in the summer of 1785.

In the bar-tabac that night Sandela said she knew Justin had been talking about her. "It's all myth, especially the stuff about me. Have you noticed how his fables tend to lead one below the belt?"

Sandela repaid his estimate of her with a critique of her own. "He's really just a failed artist himself, a latter-day expatriate who went off to Paris in the fifties, long after the best American hand had been played in France."

His work, she said, was bought, but not really felt, and his preoccupation was not his art but his school, the thing he was counting on to make his reputation. And more the pity for him, she thought, since Roussâtre had always played a poor second to the art institute in LaCoste. "Sure, he's charmed Cartier-Bresson and a few other gray lords into driving up for a lunch in the refectory. They don't really respect him. It's all for show; so the students can write their parents about the fancy elbows they're rubbing."

It was only a few days after this warning and counterwarning that Devorah led two carloads of students into Arles. On the way they passed the van from La-Coste, full of alert if conventional faces. Her own lot had gone four abreast down the town's narrowest walkways, and one of them made a loud, lewd fool of himself in a mock French accent. A boy half her age asked if she'd care to duck into a pension with him for the afternoon. Disgusted, she ordered them all back into the cars for the return to the academy. They were not chastened but surly about their interrupted outing.

That night she found a note on her door, *vous avez la communication*, unsigned. She might have thought this meant she had the message if Sandela had not helped her beyond the literal to the idiomatic "you're through."

"Someone thinks you're finished here."

She took the note to Reynolds and told him, "I don't need this aggravation. If I'm not wanted, I'll leave tomorrow."

Of course she was wanted, he said. Inevitably there would be a few problem children in a progressive institution. We have to let this sort of thing bounce off us. It would be a shame to let it spoil all the good work that can still be done.

She wasn't in the refectory the next day, when Melanie Thayer rose after the noon meal to call for a meeting of "all those who want to discuss the Devorah problem." Sandela made sure Devorah got the whole story, who had responded and how, and the indifference of most of the faculty. Perhaps some feared the attack that might come their way. That evening, Devorah rose at dinner. "Adults deal directly with one another. If you have complaints, bring them to me." There was just enough applause to save her from complete embarrassment.

What Melanie brought to class next was a canvas painted with goat dung. She called the stinking thing "the airing of a daily reality," and, as if this excused her, "a perfect color match for the field down there."

"Get it out of here," Devorah told her. "Bury it."

"Aren't you the high goddess of pigment?" Melanie came back at her. "Didn't you tell us the finest Indian yellow is made from the urine of cows fed on mango leaves?"

"The yellow is permanent," Devorah told the class slowly. "The development of a pigment is scientific, not political. This is fugitive. This is caca."

Summer

"The trouble was," Reynolds said, "they thought you made everything a chore. You're right of course, but you have to remember they pay for this. They pay a lot." He hoped she'd bend a little this session, try to have more fun. And he reminded her that one of these evenings it would be her turn to lecture the whole school. Had she thought about what she was going to say?

Her favorites, Daisy and Janelia, had gone home to Mississippi, along with most of the other first-session students. Melanie's decision to continue under Devorah's instruction puzzled her until Sandela explained.

"She comes from a pass-fail college. For all they know, the D you gave her was an A. Pelagie sent it along as a pass. You're helping her graduate."

There was the de Sade business again, and it gave Devorah the creeps—not the rake's alleged behavior, which the biography made almost forgivable, but these people's obsession with it, as if it were their own dark curse. The LaCoste school just to the east actually sat below the Marquis' château, but it was the Roussâtre academy that imagined itself in de Sade's shadow.

Unwinding again in the bar-tabac, Sandela asked what she made of the three scars on Solange's forehead. Devorah hadn't thought much about it; probably some childhood thing of little consequence, she said. She showed Sandela a thin white line on her own leg from an ages-old burn on a campfire grill. She'd never even put a salve on it. Hardly felt it, just a sting, and done.

"It doesn't take much to leave a lifelong mark."

Sandela couldn't believe this innocence.

"Oh, no" she said, "I've seen it before. I'm sure it was a cigarette to the skin three times. They're too evenly spaced to be accidental." Either Justin had delivered his wife from an early bondage, or he had branded her himself. She left Devorah obliged to accept one of these alternatives or continue naïve.

Devorah was holding firm to her method of isolating the issues.

"Today," she said, "we're going to paint the model with straight lines only. And every line must be vertical, horizontal, or a forty-five-degree diagonal. No curves." The new-session students were hidden behind their easels. She wasn't sure which of them were groaning. With this group Melanie had set out more methodically to foment insurrection, and the whining set her off again.

"You think this is bad," she told the others, "wait till she has you paint four stripes on your canvas and calls it *Landscape on a Clear Day at Four P.M.*"

"Is that all, Melanie?"

"No, I forgot, at seventy-two Fahrenheit."

Walking behind the easels she saw that Melanie and the boy beside her were both treating the subject in front of them as a montage of circles.

The question again was, Why am I here? And the only reasonable answer, Because I want to paint Provence. On her next day off she took her backpack easel into the valley and set up next to adjacent fields of sunflowers and lavender. Complementary flaming yellow and bright purple pulsed against each other under the high July sun. The colors seemed to jump out of the ground. She found it unbelievable, unpaintable. All the brightness, all the heat was insupportable. Her breath was short. Dejected, she packed up everything, and taking deep breaths, began the long steep trek to the school on the cliffs.

Perhaps halfway home, she stopped and looked back, hoping to take heart from the distance she had already come. Against the darker rolling fields was a farmhouse, perhaps half a mile below her. She could see at least five shades of ochre on its multiple roofs and walls, a complex that must have grown over the years, and weathered into this beautiful and muted sequence of yellow, orange, red, and shadow. This was hers!

She set her easel up again and fastened her canvas. She began to block in the shapes. Everything in order and going quite mechanically, she worked in silence. Five times she mixed for the five shades between yellow and red; and five times she watched her palette knife disappear against the background color. The walls were up, the roofs were on. The browns and duns of the rolling fields and hills beyond were treated with the same loving care. She was little more than an hour at this; then done!

But nothing. It seemed dead to her. Not at all what she saw across the valley. She grabbed her palette knife and began to scrape. Obliterating this line and that, until walls and roofs began to blur. In the middle of this destructive fit she stood back from the easel for a new perspective and it came to her. She wasn't destroying the work at all. In fact, the picture was beginning to resemble what her eyes perceived at a half mile's distance.

She began to touch it here and there, compromising with the geometrical truth of lines and separations until they became as real to her as her eye's original discovery. The patchwork of ochres was a rambling farmhouse with its own centuries-old story—a sequence and rhythm of construction, color, and weathering. To retell that story with any truthfulness, you might begin with nameable colors, she imagined herself telling an attentive class, but you never finish with them. Don't be fooled by your first static response. Of course she had known this before—that there must be movement and allowance for the eye's deception if there is to be life—but it had never come home to her before in this decisive fashion.

There was a grand difference between what her intellect told her she must be seeing and what she actually saw. The nameable truth always gave way to the reassessing game of the eye. She climbed back to the village, pleased with herself, ready to share her new excitement with the school. And the next day she began, "don't imagine what you see, just see."

The next thing she saw was Melanie casually removing her clothes in the middle of the terrace, and easing the model off her seat. "Can't you be more natural?"

Melanie was asking the woman, who did not speak English. "Like this." She straddled the chair, draping her arms over its ladder back, and extended a leg, admiring its length. Twisting the whole thing from the hip, she said, "I have a dancer's turnout."

Not satisfied with that, she climbed onto a table and took a pretzel pose in which her arm circled under a raised leg, and reached up to give lift to her heavy breast. She looked at all of them as if to ask, Well, why don't you get started? Devorah kicked a leg of the table and Melanie tumbled onto her side. She left the terrace hugging her bundle of clothes.

Later that morning Devorah went to tell Justin that Melanie was no longer welcome in her class. He was waiting for her with Solange behind the altar screen. Sandela and Melanie were just on their way out, the two of them having a good laugh until they saw her, and sobered as if obliged in her presence to show respect for the academy's inner sanctum.

Justin called Melanie's behavior "an impulse thing" and was satisfied to leave it at that. "She creates these scenes because she needs something to brood about. I suppose I ought to put something in our rule book." But rules, he reminded Devorah, were symptoms of institutional insecurity. "And we don't want to tie the creative hand."

"Please," she said, "there's been no evidence of creativity in Melanie's hand, much less her mind, or any other part of her."

Reynolds looked to his wife for support, but her head was lowered in her own thoughts, revealing again the three white circles, more prominent now against the summer-darkened skin of her forehead. This might be Reynolds' school, but Devorah would not be persuaded to give Melanie another passing grade.

In the afternoon Melanie was back on the terrace singing to herself as she painted. It was an irritating chant of self-satisfaction, as if she were coaxing her work toward art with a two-note plainsong. She'd started the canvas with bright and promising contrasts; now it was all being dulled with mindless stroking. There was no telling what she was getting at, the model, the landscape, or something beyond the physical world.

"This and that, and this and that," she sang.

Devorah was thinking of the paragraph she would write to accompany the F coming the girl's way. *Like a child, Melanie still paints from the tube. She has scant knowledge of pigment. No sense of rhythm or the ordering of shapes. No sense of weight, counterbalance, movement, or gesture. She is imitative and has meager drawing skills. Perhaps this student should turn to another pursuit.*

Instead of keeping all this to herself, Devorah made the mistake of sharing it with Sandela in the bar-tabac. She might have known the news would have a way of leaking through the most earnest vow of silence to circulate among the students, while the sunflowers and lavender fell to sickles in the valley, and there the earth relaxed again into an effortless brown behind the tan stubble of the severed shoots.

"You're the one who's failed!" Melanie screamed at her. "What have you produced here? A few useless exercises. Nothing!"

The girl took no guidance and no one but Devorah offered any. Coming up the cobbled street to the school courtyard she watched Melanie playfully grab at Sandela's behind. Her hand was slapped away, but nothing was said, as if this might be expected from one of the academy's young artists.

Fall

This time there was the same faculty, but all new students. A new and calmer Melanie had been packed off to Arles for the coming season. She hadn't been dismissed actually; Reynolds was going to be her advisor, checking up on her work from time to time. Before she left she informed Devorah she would rent her own room, work from *real* life, and paint what *she* felt.

The dusty browns of August were gradually overtaken by vineyards going orange on their way to brilliant red, with orchards in competing flame. In the second week of the new term someone entered Devorah's room and left a crude pastel torso on her hand mirror. She was trying to be softer this term, but the students still bridled at her restrictive lessons, even as they recognized the skill in her quick, wise sketches. It was no secret that of all the instructors, she was the one with a grand store of talent, the one who might actually survive someday by her painting alone. Again she told her class "I teach by isolating the issues." And again she warned them not to be unduly influenced by the nameable color.

"I want you to do a painting," she told them, "in which there is no preconceived color. Everything light should be yellow; everything middle, blue; and everything dark, a dark red."

"If there's no nameable color," she was asked, "can there be a nameable subject?"

"Of course," she snapped.

She was losing their interest again, felt herself disappearing before their eyes. And back in her room, after this unsettling class, she found there had been another invasion of her quarters. Two pages had been tucked under her pillow. At the top of one she read, "D'Eclanton, Letters From My Cell, A Translation." On each sheet there were passages highlighted with a yellow marker:

> Our monastery was a little republic, self-governed, independent of Rome and Royalty. We served the Lord with glass, tapestry, and canvas, all colored with the dyes of our own earth. The work decorating our walls was a secret from the world, not for sale or reputation, only to enrich our own lives.

We worked and loved well, and purely until the arrival of Sister Jeanne. It was I who allowed her a daily passage under the wall. She was not the first woman who had gone to her hands and knees to paint with us, but the first to find fault in our method and habit, and the first to tattle outside the gates when we ignored her interfering advice. The mystery of her death was never solved. Within our walls it was considered the just reward of a cat, which had scratched its way to hell.

To Devorah it sounded like something out of Reynolds' imagination. When she confronted him, he agreed something had to be done; this had been carried too far.

"Get back to work," he told her. "I'll put an end to it."

The next day she began her class calmly enough, lecturing again on pigment and permanence, and asking the students to produce a color match with one of the tiled roofs of the village visible from the terrace. There were no complaints, but no perfect matches either, and no special eagerness to succeed. As a group, they were perhaps more indolent than the last. In the middle of this feckless effort one of the young men asked her, "Do you think any one of us will succeed as a painter? I mean actually be famous past our own lifetime?" Her voice rose from irritation to anger, and ran away with her.

"If you want to know what's worthwhile in Western art, get yourselves to the Prado and kneel before Velazquez! Study what he passed along to Sargent! The paradox of precise rendering by mere suggestion. Miraculous strokes! Your abstractions are no more than designs. Riddles, if they're anything at all! Do you understand?"

She heard herself yelling at them.

"Riddles have answers! Art treats mysteries!"

They looked away, and down, and she understood they were embarrassed, not for themselves, but for her. She had nothing more to tell them.

"Just paint," she said. "Whatever you like."

In her mailbox she found a postcard from Melanie in Arles. The picture was an eighteenth-century Dutch drawing of two grinning boys dressed in knickers and puffed sleeves. Between them they carried a black cat hanging by its feet from a pole. The message was brief: "Did you know torture used to be good sport? Will you be coming back to the academy next year?" No return address, only the Arles postmark.

Devorah longed for a worthy correspondent. She sat down and wrote to Baltimore, more to the city than to the fickle man there who, now that she was absent, begged for news, which would only have bored him if she spoke it to his face. She wrote that things were becoming ghoulish, explaining the D'Eclanton papers and the de Sade biography that she'd been reading by default.

. . . here, in this countryside where de Sade fed peasant girls on dangerous doses of a liquorice compound in hopes of intoxicating himself on the wind they might pass in his face. You might think latter-day perversions would pale by comparison.

I've considered leaving before my contract expires, but I'm sure the director here would repay me with poor references if I tried for a job in the university system. The drawing instructor has attached herself to me as if we were a sorority of two, full of secrets and superiority. She tells me the others here consider my work "showy." I've offended everyone. The teaching I have to offer belittles them all. You asked me for local color. That's easy. The lumpy landscape of the village is in fact a chalky pigment. Children playing on the cliffs come home stained orange and yellow.

In the last weeks of the session her students listened without interest. Often they got right to work on their own, maybe fearing another of Devorah's outbursts would leave them no room at all for their own inclinations. Another page of the D'Eclanton account was slipped under her door, this one a description of the interfering Sister's body after her fall from the Roussâtre cliffs, and the perfunctory sympathy in the memorial service performed by the Brothers of the Little Gate.

She thought of leaving immediately, without giving notice.

She could imagine a modern crime in these walls going unreported and unpunished, as easily rationalized as D'Eclanton's story.

Sandela reminded her that was a different century. And D'Eclanton's cell was in the Bastille, in earshot of the Marquis' raving. "D'Eclanton," she said, "was only in for blasphemy."

"And murder. But I thought you said this was all bogus."

"Oh, I don't know. Listen, Justin wants your painting of the farm to hang with the academy's permanent collection." A rare honor, she explained. "He's never even hung one of his own."

"Well, he's not getting one of mine. Why doesn't he ask me?"

"He doesn't know how much you'd expect for it." But there was something else she wanted. Could Devorah cover for her on the coming weekend? Sandela was hoping for a little time to be alone, though it was her turn to keep a watch on the dormitory. No, Devorah said, she'd promised herself time off with her easel and paints again. She meant to find a city marketplace and let her eye lead wherever it would.

Sandela was nodding, as if something had been settled at last, perhaps the limits of their friendship.

Later, feeling a bit selfish, Devorah went to Sandela's room and said she had reconsidered. Not about the weekend, but about the painting.

"Tell Reynolds he can have it. I mean if he'll just come and ask me for it." And he did, that very night. It was already on stretchers. She'd imagined there might be some ceremony of transfer, but he came for it without delay, and said he would take it for framing that weekend. He took it right out of her hands.

"Gorgeous," he said. "You've taught us something, and now you're leaving the lesson with us. Wonderful!"

"What lesson is that?"

She was sure he'd be at a loss to give precision to the vague compliment. She was wrong. She heard the words of the lecture she'd given to the school repeated as if he were reading from her notes.

"In order to achieve a semblance of reality, we tell a lie, we lie against the moment. We paint the process of seeing."

It was cunning, the guile behind his furrowed brow. She was already sorry she'd changed her mind. She didn't feel any safer in her room for having shown her generosity, only a little shamed by Sandela, a little used.

Her sleep that night was interrupted by a vision of the man she had written to in Baltimore, a recollection of his tampering with her car's engine to prolong a country weekend. Here she imagined more than tampering— like someone releasing the brake, and letting her VW roll across the parking terrace, right over the cliff, where the only restraint was a little sign that said *Prennez les Mains des Enfants*, Hold Your Children's Hands.

The next morning, as if she had willed her car out of commission with her own anxiety, it would not start. A change of plans. She rode into Apt with the chummy busboys Roger and Molan, to paint in the centuries-old Saturday market. The boys' enthusiasm for her company lasted only until their arrival in the town. They let her off several blocks from the market, and told her to meet them at the same corner for the return trip in the evening.

"Will you do my portrait?" Roger asked. It was a joke, and meant to insult her. She knew they supposed it was a task beyond her ability, a job for an artist, not a teacher.

"Yes, for his mother," called Molan. "*Bonne chance!* Sell a picture. Help with the gas!"

They left her to find her own way.

Farmers with their trade in carts and on their backs led her toward the market center. With her folding easel on shoulder straps, she felt like one of them, though her sweatshirt and blue jeans marked her clearly as American. She was quickly engulfed in the wider frenzy of selfish concerns. If they took notice it was only for the quicker pleasure of ignoring her.

She saw the labor and product of the whole region displayed on these few acres of ancient Roman cobble: the previous week's urine, guano, blood, scales, and withered greens barely washed away, and now a fresh delivery of the same plenty to sell in a day or be lost. It was that way with painting *en pleine air* too; catch the light in time or lose it.

Underfoot, she recognized a sliver of squid cartilage, like translucent plastic. She picked it up and stared through it, refracting the market stalls all across the square, bending the light over everything that could be harvested, dug, or picked; baked, pickled, confected; snared, shot, netted, or hooked. And beyond these, a bazaar of all that could be tinkered, stitched, joined, or cobbled. She was thinking this must be what she had come for, this fresh and filthy market. Full of life, mold, nourishment, bacteria, flavor. Her America, paved and inspected, could not have this, would not tolerate it. She felt superior to her countrymen, who supposed that what was sealed under plastic would be safer than what spoiled under the sun. Something here was worth capturing, worth taking home.

There wasn't time to see it all. The delights stretched away in every direction. She was eager to set up and begin. Each new hour destroyed the last, changing the color of every visible plane. Holding herself at a remove from the commotion, she chose a face behind a fish stall. In its contours she saw steel dignity and the hollows of aging. But she must see without staring. "Mustn't spook the trout," as she told her students.

The scream of a hare shot through the charcoal smoke. For an instant her whole career seemed defeated by the dun stippling on a single mushroom. People were gathering around her easel to watch as she blocked in the larger shapes of the composition. They were waiting for reality, and so far there was nothing to admire. She heard skepticism in their voices, and then pity. Before moving on they needed proof she was a painter.

"Ah!"

A murmur of comprehension as the fishwife's mouth opened on the canvas, as red and black as the mackerel under her knife. Freed from doubt, Devorah's strokes began to reveal the market's mood in quantum jumps. A daub here set the angle of a neck and became a haggler's attitude. Another there gave the answering contempt in the gesture of the merchant's hand. There was a conversation of appreciation behind her as she stepped back to admire what was happening on the canvas.

From there the work moved quickly, with Devorah floating along on happy discoveries. The faces on the canvas were surprising her as well, coming alive with the energy of barter and dispute. She was performing for her audience now, and they coaxed her on with muttered affirmation. She was almost finished when a man walked out of the crowd and made an offer unique in her experience: he wanted to buy the painting right off the easel. And he offered her five hundred dollars for it. An American with far too much money, showing off. She refused him. He offered a thousand. She refused again, thinking, *am I crazy?* Had it been a

Frenchman, she would have accepted in an instant. But this was too vulgar, too demeaning, with his woman begging beside him.

"Get it for me! Oh, you must, David! Get it for me. Puleeeese!"

Finished, she did not roll the wet canvas but carried it by the edge, walking out of the marketplace and through the streets, asking for directions, till she came to a small gallery and framing shop that would hold it for her return. She gave awkward instructions, repeating herself until she was certain the man understood it was not to be sold. Then off to toast herself and her first victory in France.

Each trade and avocation had its own bar in Apt. After the mistake of a soda water in the Café des Bicyclistes, Devorah was shown the way to Charbon des Artistes, where the city's painters and gallery operators gathered. The walls of its crowded rooms had been given over to Vasarely and his imitators. As if the popular urban folk art hadn't wall space enough in every corner of France. Straight edge and compass, she called it; nothing but design, nothing but riddle. The place was quiet for all the drinking in progress, full of earnest talk of politics and painters. She hadn't been in the bar more than a moment when, under a childish pattern of solid colors on the far wall, her eyes were drawn down to the surreal, the impossible—two familiar heads in the booth below, the gray mane of Justin Reynolds tangled with the black hair and very likeness of Sandela

Marks. Devorah couldn't credit what she saw, forehead to forehead, and arms linked on the table between them, fingers twined. A moment later Solange and Melanie Thayer, hand in hand and flushed red, came out of the hall from a back room and joined them.

Sidling along the far side of the bar, Devorah circled behind them. The miscoupling had corrected itself; Solange was sitting beside her husband, who was whispering in her ear, and Melanie had settled into conversation with Sandela on their side of the booth. One by one, from her hidden vantage, Devorah examined the faces of all four, considering their deceit, the same four who entailed her life in the academy: Solange the paymaster, and Reynolds, who appeased, Sandela the intriguer, and Melanie, who whined and provoked. Still unseen, she believed, hidden by the crowd and a wooden partition, she ducked into the booth behind them, lowering her head to the table, cocking her ear.

Justin was saying he thought the new semester was going quite well "thanks to our saint from Baltimore."

"Why can't she spell it *Deborah* like everyone else?" Melanie asked.

She could hear Sandela say the problem is self-importance. "Devorah is humorless."

"No!" Justin interrupted, his voice clear over the hum of the crowd. "You're both wrong. Devorah's all right. Fundamentals. Discipline."

"Yes," Solange went on. "All the indulgence. All that painting from the tube. It had to change. Don't roll your eyes at me, Melanie."

"Painting from the tube?" Melanie asked. "What's with the trendy mouth? You're talking like her."

"No, Melanie, you could have learned a lot from Devorah. She's a very generous instructor. And what are you laughing about, Sandela?"

Justin and his wife were coming to her defense as they'd never done in her presence. She might have left it at that and snuck off savoring the unexpected endorsement, but the praise was too easily offered; something was wrong. Melanie changed the subject to the rest of the weekend. "One room or two tonight? Because I'm not sleeping with—"

"What are you talking about?" Justin cut her off. "No, Devorah's doing just fine. We want her back next year. We'll make it worth her while."

"She's a stone bitch, Justin. You said—"

"Melanie, that's not so. I never—"

"Just today, you said," she insisted.

"Since when did you start calling him Justin?" Solange asked.

"Since forever," Melanie said, "as if . . . get your hand off my knee."

Devorah began to feel sullied by her spying. It suddenly occurred to her that Justin must have seen her entering the bar. He would have warned Solange. The two of them were using Sandela and Melanie as foils, aware that Devorah could be listening behind the partition. She rose from her hiding place, and stood over them.

"Imagine!" Justin said, jumping up. "Devorah, your ears must be burning. Sit with us."

"Do you know what this means for your school?" she said.

She felt her hand shaking, reaching out to the table to steady herself. "You're going down!" she said, her voice rising. "All of you!" The people at the next table began to stare. Heads turned across the room. The maître d' shook a warning finger in their direction and came out from behind the bar.

"Freaks!" she yelled at them.

"Devorah!" Justin began again, ignoring everything she'd said. "Imagine you here! What fun!"

"Aren't you well?" Sandela asked.

"Here, sit with us," Solange was urging, scrunching over against her husband. "Something has happened. Tell us."

"You've happened! That's what's happened! Sandela, I thought you were looking for some time to be alone this weekend."

"Oh, let up," Sandela said.

"Let up? She's a student!" Devorah was pointing at Melanie. She felt a tug at her shoulder. The maître d' had hold of her arm.

"This is not possible," he said. "Outside please, if you must, this way."

"Who are you?" she turned on him.

"Monsieur Repholt. Please, outside."

"Look here, Repholt. Look at these people," she said. "They call themselves an art academy."

"Devorah, stop," Reynolds ordered her, "you've misunderstood this."

"We'll take care of her," he told the maître d'. "Something's upset her," but the man held fast to Devorah's arm.

"That's the director," she told him. "He tells his students they're too modest, that modesty blocks their talent and blights their lives. Very convenient. He grooms the saucy ones for Madame Pelagie there. Creative freedom, they call it."

Justin tried to stand. Solange pulled him back.

Devorah had the attention of half the room. If she stopped now, it could only be a retreat into shame and embarrassment. "Everyone," she said, "this is Justin Reynolds and his wife, Madame Pelagie. And this is their little trick, Melanie. Look at her. Her parents paid five thousand dollars for this. And this one, this is her favorite instructor."

"Enough!" Repholt said. "Come away."

"It's all right," Justin told him. "Let go of her. She's confused."

"This man," she said, pointing at Reynolds again, "lunches with your Minister of Culture. Students come all the way from America to his little school on the cliff. He fills them with fairy tales, and that's not all—"

"You've lost the plot," Justin told her. "They don't know what you're talking about. You're making a fool of yourself."

She was being hauled away by Repholt and a man from the kitchen.

They didn't need to drag her any farther. Devorah was finished. She'd meant to give them a lecture they'd never forget. But it was like trying to paint the pulsing landscape of sunflowers and lavender when all it brought to mind were the simplest, vulgar colors on her palette. The academy's controlling ménage was unpaintable. Pulling free, she called back at them.

"Screw you!"

She took herself to the doorway and into the street. Hurrying away, she thought they might follow and try to silence her, because she was on her way to tell anyone who'd listen just what was happening at the American Academy in Roussâtre.

In the streets of Apt she made a large circle out of straight lines, and came in good time to the corner where Roger and Molan were supposed to meet her. The boys had forgotten their promise. It was long after dark when she found a bus that would take her into the country, within walking distance of the monastery. As she hiked the last steep kilometer, she was already making plans for an early departure.

In her mail slot there was another *vous avez la communication*. This time the note was decorated with a latrine scribble of a vagina.

She stomped up to her room, not caring if she woke the whole place. She had just changed into her nightshirt and slippers when she saw another typed page had been left on her bed. More of the D'Eclanton diary.

Nothing more was heard from Sister Jeanne. There was the garrote, and she breathed no more. Of course I, already accused as an enemy of the church, would be the magistrate's target. Hadn't a hundred brothers heard me announce from the refectory dais that her tattling tongue would soon be in the devil's care?

Devorah sent the note and page sailing out her window, down onto the sleeping village. She was packing her little carryall only with essentials. Sweater, blouse, extra jeans, a change of underwear, passport. And, she hoped, enough francs to get her to Paris, but first to Apt, where she'd pick up her painting of the marketplace. They could have the rest—her clothes, her easel, and the VW that wasn't worth its sales tax.

Slowly she began to change. Coming out of the nightshirt, arms overhead at the mirror, she was reassured not so much by the solidity of her reflection as the righteousness that held her erect before the glass, the determination of her mission. "I'm out of here," she said. A voice that seemed to be coming through the ceiling was agreeing with her.

"You're history," it said.

There were footfalls through an upper corridor, muffled voices, a scurrying away. Her eyes followed across the ceiling along a crack to a small hole in the plaster. Voyeurs as well? Had they been watching her at her morning and evening toilet, her naked stretching at the armoire glass? She was thinking Reynolds might try to silence her before she could tattle to the world. Dressed again in jersey, jeans, and sandals, she grabbed her bag and hurried down through the stone passage into the night.

Was it the echo of her own steps she heard in the narrow alley, or was someone actually coming after her? A light shined up through the town gate. She ran from the beam, down the path to the monk's gate, and left Roussâtre on all fours, going under the wall, just as she'd arrived. She must stay off the road, she thought, at least for the night. When she reached the fields at the bottom of the mountain, she lay down exhausted, and slept under the stars.

At dawn, moving beside a windbreak of poplar trees, she was almost at the valley road when she startled a squatting farmer. He shook an angry finger at her and called her something she translated as "painted woman." Her forearms and neck were covered with orange dust from the night before. Rubbing it ground it deeper into her skin.

Baltimore

Devorah came home with neither of her favorite French paintings. She'd been duped into giving away the farmhouse treatment and the marketplace scene had been sold against her instructions. The proprietor of the frame shop said his wife had misunderstood and taken two hundred dollars for the canvas only an hour after she'd left it. The American who bought it had thrown bills from his wallet like a fool, his woman pleading for the painting. And what was he to do?

"But what good luck for you! Look, your money!"

She had been furious; this man had cheated her as well, lying about the price. She set off for Paris, taking buses from one hostel to the next, more like a gypsy than a woman returning to a fixed life. The skin on her neck was like a gypsy's, too, blotchy with the ochre. At first she had tried wetting her fingers with saliva and rubbing at it, which only seemed to brighten the stain. The more she rubbed, the more enflamed it became. By the time she reached Baltimore it was like a painted sore. On the plane from Paris she must have used the lavatory a dozen times or more—not the toilet but the mirror. The fluorescent light over the vanity made it look as if she'd been birthmarked with Mercurochrome.

Devorah shared the story of her tour in France with a woman named Delores who sat beside her in the window seat, choosing her words carefully, rehearsing for when it would matter, when the appropriate people would be contacted about the whole sorry condition of the academy. She imagined a firm but discreet role for herself in bringing down Reynolds and perhaps his school with him. If he remained the director, why should the place survive?

Delores listened quietly. She was somber as her name, but the wrong audience for scandal. "What is it you actually saw?" she asked. "The younger woman holding the lady's hand? That might be rather sweet. Convention is so cruel to older women." Devorah turned away. She was thinking of the flushed faces of Solange and Melanie as they came hand in hand from a back room, patent proof of their lubricious tryst, and quite useless as evidence against them.

At home there was a pile of mail waiting, the expected stack of catalogues, and a dozen or more personal letters, one of them from Roussâtre, which she saved for last. The first she opened was from the father of one of the girls she'd taught in the summer session. He identified himself as a sustaining patron of the academy, an admirer of hers through the proxy of his daughter. Sorry to hear of the nervous affliction that struck her, he doubted the school could give her financial aid in the event therapeutic intervention was necessary, or hospitalization. He might consider his private support. She dropped this into her wastebasket and went on to the next.

An old classmate of hers from the Maryland Institute was anxious to communicate. He'd heard of her trouble through one of their mutual teachers. He had been through emotional turmoil of his own, a serious depression, and might have some things to share. "It's all drugs these days," he wrote. "They're not half bad."

She grabbed the first letter to rip it up with this one, and took up the next, something official by the look of it. Under a list of partners and associates, a note from Reynolds' lawyer in Manhattan.

My client Justin Reynolds hopes to be in direct correspondence with you shortly. In the meantime he has asked me to forward this certified letter, extending his sympathy for the strain of your recent employment at his academy in Roussâtre.

My firm is normally retained for overview of contractual matters, but Mr. Reynolds wished me to explain that we are also ready to protect the reputations of the art school, its principals and its acting staff against defamation, written or spoken. In case I may be of service to you in this regard,

I am very sincerely,

After this she went straight to the letter from Justin, actually a memo with enclosure.

To our fugitive color, Devvy:

Farmer Pagnol, the one you caught with his pants down, said you were on your way to Paris! Sandela told us how frightened you must have been. I wish you had come to me. We think we know who the troublemakers were, and you can be sure they won't be coming back here again.

I'm still not sure what caused your moment in the café. We were so pleased to see you, and then, boom! You know we were allowing Melanie Thayer to live and work in Arles for the session. We were meeting in Apt to check up on her progress since we were still responsible for her.

I doubt we could talk you into returning for another session, but in case you should want to teach in an American university feel free to use the enclosed. Of course I'd be glad to write to anyone directly about your obvious qualifications.

Devorah turned to his endorsement.

Miss Francke came to us in the spring of 1986, adding vitality and quality to our staff of professional instructors. Rather than comment on her painting skills, which will be evident from her slides, I would commend her energy and uplifting vision. She was as demanding with herself as with our students. Her teaching method elicited surprising work from beginners, and sophisticated responses from students of advanced talent. She was a forceful and articulate champion of the figurative, and an enemy of the modern complacence with self-expression. She will be an asset on any art faculty.

There was more about her painting exercises, the tutorial approach to space, solidity, and harmony. Reynolds, who had never sat through one of her classes, had struck every note to please her.

She imagined a reply: *Do you think I don't understand what chance a champion of the figurative has today? What chance an enemy of complacent self-expression has at any college or university in America? Do you think I'd want a recommendation from you, that I don't know what was happening in Apt? Do you think the stone walls of your monastery can hold your ugly secret?*

Her anger turned to disgust. Eventually disgust gave way to depression and impotence. As soon as she left that bar in Apt, Justin must have gone to work, warning the academy and appropriate friends in America about the delusional woman coming their way. What good was her testimony against this practiced charlatan? Who'd believe her against the campaign of innocence already under way?

No, her silence might be more effective than the charges he would dodge and hurl back. She called no one, she wrote no exposé. She prepared no résumés. She was steering clear of university art faculties. The tales from Roussâtre stayed within the walls of her own studio, where she began to teach again with her old success.

Melanie naked, Melanie painting with shit, the three-scarred forehead of Madame Pelagie, and Director Reynolds' moveable ménage: these became the apocryphal lore of Devorah's Loft, a comical mythology that intrigued the students, who pressed her for details. She knew they thought it was largely her invention.

Devorah had to be told by friends and finally a dermatologist that if she stopped rubbing the places on her neck and arms, the redness would go away. The story would not. A few years later she heard the American Academy in Roussâtre was flourishing. By then it was associated with two major universities and supported by a well-heeled foundation. The founding director, Reynolds, pleased with his life's project, had taken the emeritus mantle, living close by in France with his wife, and enjoying the school's perquisites to paint and share the life of the students.

A few years later she no longer had to teach. Lucien Freud and the figurative were in fashion. A critic said Devorah was reaching toward Sargent, a worthy if unattainable goal. Her painting was supporting her. She was taking only a few students by then, and when they asked her about the academy in France, it was a chance to explain again that every pigment had its unique history and its own longevity—a chance to pull a torn jersey from the closet and demonstrate once more the tenacity of Roussâtre ochre. At least that was the nameable color.

Had these women fallen into
the rest of France as well?

3

The Doll House

PART ONE

Transgression

Father Anthonie, curé in the Pyrenees village of
Gontrin, in his late sixties, had looked forward to the
satisfactions of a just life—contentment with his
celibacy and the gathered wisdom of myriad confes-
sions, the confidence of his bishop, along with the respect and devotion of his congregation. Instead he was
troubled with the anxiety of failure. The arc of life on
its downward turn was taking his pleasure and his
honor down with it, leading him to clerical excess.

Things were backward. As his appetite grew and was obliged, his weight fell. Pallor and sunken cheeks diminished the glad face he intended for his morning mirror. He was more alive at night than when he woke in the morning. Sleep could exhaust him. There was flushing, too, and an occasional arrhythmia. A doctor from Carcassonne diagnosed apnea, a condition that stole one's breath in the night, robbing the brain and heart of oxygen.

Again he'd chosen the wrong housekeeper, a man this time, after the discharge of an interfering lady puffed up with her indispensability. In Cecil he found more than he'd wanted. He was the kind who had to be told "enough!" to discourage hovering, or move him out of a room.

It was a relief to have no more insolent comment on the condition of his underwear, and no more yelling from kitchen to the dining table, but now there were garlic potions forced on his colds, and Cecil's showy masculine energy, which could break a plate or a lamp, and provoke the curé to unchristian muttering. He was muttering as he made his daily entry in the parish log: while dusting, Cecil smashed the ceramic frame with storks made by my mother. Sweeping up the pieces with the photo of my ordination day, he asked how much it cost. *Eh bien.* Henri Pons has disappeared. His wife seems not much concerned.

——✴✴——

Afraid of the impression that might be given by two men in close quarters, the father had not allowed Cecil to spend nights in the parsonage as the departed woman had sometimes done. He thought it just as well that three times a week Cecil took the bus to Prades, where he had alternate work Tuesdays, Thursdays, and Saturdays, keeping things tidy somewhere else. When he took his apron off, he looked to the father like a city hustler in his tight blue pants and purple shirt.

It seemed remarkable that Cecil had one of the village's few telephones. Still more surprising in the little community of shepherds and weavers was the computer he'd brought home from a trip to the city. With this, it was said, he made contact with the world at large in a way new and puzzling to most of Gontrin, including the curé, who was aware that men sometimes gathered in his housekeeper's cottage to watch the machine perform its electric tricks.

Cecil had always been thought of as the backward child of a backward family beholden by their demanding faith to making too many babies. Cecil was the seventh of ten. But where had the worldliness come from? Where had he learned his alphabet, and how did his thick fingers manage on the computer's letter board? He explained to the father that his equipment was old and very slow. Really, you could find such an antique thing in the city's discards, with the thinking already inside it. His machine cost him nothing.

"But I've heard you can wander anywhere in the world," the curé said.

"Yes, Father, but not quickly, not with my old modem."

He was damned if he'd ask the man what a modem was. What did it matter anyway? Like this, the curé's attitude toward his man could shift from resignation to curiosity to a blasphemous anger. If it were not so close to the last firing, he'd be inclined to discharge Cecil, too. And if he hadn't believed that negative fantasies were a sinful indulgence, he might have dwelled on a suspicion that the man had been subtly placed by the bishop to report on his failings. This was the new bishop, who complained that Father Anthonie trudged behind the modern pace.

It was true the curé of Gontrin lived much in the past. He took his history seriously, and not just the Bible. His reading on the Cathar heresy, for example, which gave him a message for these wandering souls in his care, and a scheme to get at something sinister. A man was missing from the village. After the Feast Day service the father walked the center aisle of his church, nodding and pointing at the young people expected to remain when the others left the sanctuary.

"You . . . and you . . . and you," he said. "You needn't stay, Cecil."

Defying his wish, his housekeeper remained in his forward pew, pious to a fault. As for the rest of them, he was sorry for these and all the children of the new age, a generation that had come to doubt mystical truth, because machines like Cecil's gave science dominion. Reaching the back of the church, he gazed through the open doors at the crystalline heaven over the mountains. An otherwise perfect sky was sliced in half by the vapor trail of a jet plane inching eastward toward the Mediterranean Sea. He'd been told these planes could change the weather, and believed he had seen it happen. The wispy trails turned into full clouds, the clouds darkened, and the rain fell. It was science up to tricks, dealing a god's mixed hand, soaking one man's Feast Day, and another's parched field.

He turned back to his chosen dozen in the church. They'd be thinking it was time for his annual message on the familiar struggle—their battle with the prime temptation. He expected a little fuss, but there was no argument from parents whose nostrils had turned in the direction of lamb roasting at the village center, and the people's vat, bung already dripping to those who had turned their backs on the morning Mass.

Under surplice, cassock, blouse, and a full body stocking of wool, none of them fitting quite properly on his shrunken body, the curé was not overdressed in the chilly nave. In fact it was a perspiration of worry soaking through to the folds of white linen under his arms. A man had gone missing, and these young people whispered of it in a sly gossip.

"The body is in a closet."

He'd heard that much in a morning confession. "Who? Where?"

"I can't say," a veiled woman known perfectly well to him whispered back through the wooden bars.

As she left, he'd cracked the door of the confessional and seen her whispering to others waiting their turn with him. It made him bolder now, but none of the twelve picked to receive his lecture—seven male, five female—seemed chastened by their selection. A couple of them were preening in their new status as likely sinners; in particular, the Boret child, Rixende, the youngest of them at twelve, already heavy of thigh, with eyes questing, and whose mother favored her inclusion here. It seemed less a blushing shame for Rixende than a startling acknowledgment of her eligibility, and she twisted in her seat to see who remained in the church to witness her arrival.

Cecil's head was moving forward and back in a steady rhythm, needlessly affirming the father's every word. The curé might have ignored this except that everything he was saying would be heard by this silly man and perhaps passed along with the rest of the trivia he confided to his computer, maybe to be sent out as news of the world—news that could move in any direction. And Cecil would be noticing the disrespect of these young people.

Start with Roland Malet, who was gazing upward, counting the ceiling timbers as he might count the years he'd heard the same preachments—seven. At eighteen Roland had fathered a child in Prades, and now twenty, continued his irresponsible way here in Gontrin, trading on his family's good name.

Briefly a shepherd, discharged for sleep at duty, Roland was hired with bed and board by the farmer Jauffre, who kept a sharp eye for the conduct of his daughter Charlotte (also here), but paid no mind to the boy after work and dinner, when he should have climbed to his bed in the loft. Allowed no lantern in the barn, Roland was expected to keep the hours of the sun, yet the curé and the whole village knew how he went lurking about after dark.

Jacotte Pons, turning her face from the curé, was the one most stung by her detention in the church. He could sense that. Her heart would be racing in fear of what he might know and say. Afraid he might force her to speak and deny, that she might have to stand, short and stout, stammering in front of these immoderate young with whom she had so little in common. A grown woman, after all! But if she were innocent, she could easily have said, "It's my husband who has disappeared. What right have you to shame me?"

Perhaps he could make her confess right here. The truth could be spread with guests of the feast all the way to Carcassonne. The bishop there might have his mind opened, might even take the occasional friendly visit to Gontrin as the previous bishop had, to cadge a brandy, and spend an afternoon begging the temper of the people from the curé. For that one, hadn't he explained the rages of the young from the anarchy of the film star Belmondo to the scandal of a half-naked, singing Madonna?

He had tapped Jacotte on the shoulder, and said for the whole church to hear, *"Vous aussi."*

It was one of his favorite cautions that "one thing leads to another," so simple and trite, he knew. They could despise, but not argue with it.

Sitting directly behind Jacotte was Christophe, the Spanish count's shepherd, recently here from south of the mountains with his black curls, and lips swollen with a lusty desire. He was grazing in Gontrin with the impunity of his flock. Leaning forward, he cooed close to Jacotte's ear; maybe his notion of an audible balm for her embarrassment.

The detained twelve, excluding Christophe, who was new to this, would be expecting the traditional rebuke—"Don't think I don't know which of you are already on your way to hell."

Instead he said softly, and with a calculated grief, "Eight hundred years ago . . . "

They couldn't have been more surprised by this turn than if he'd begun "Once upon a time . . . "

He had a story of heresy and charred flesh that would chill the blood of these children who schemed today, or worse, in ignorance of villagers who, for their faith, had perished in a single day—neighbors of their forefathers in Gontrin. A man is missing; that's the point. There are people here who know where a body is hidden.

This is mixed in the father's mind with his reading of the city scholar's history of the Cathar counterfaith in the ancient fortified villages on this north slope of the mountains, and the walled city of the plain below. A contagion had spread up through the hills and valleys. And within this centuries-old story was the account of another missing man. Father Anthonie believed it was no accident he had read this in time to confront Jacotte.

He was struck by the bravery of the old heretics, and troubled in his faith by their apt argument. They believed in twin forces, a righteous God in heaven and an evil God on earth. The evidence in Gontrin still pointed that way. Witness today, with foul play afoot. As for the migration of souls—the evil ones taking residence in animal fetuses, and the pure in the wombs of pregnant women—well, he did believe there were souls taking temporary refuge here and there; not doomed, but not yet worthy of salvation.

There was Cecil's head, still bobbing like a metronome, a nagging insistence on a rhythm for the father's delivery, and an insinuation: get to the point.

"Rixende, sit up! That's not a bed."

The girl sneered, in danger, he thought, of becoming the slut her mother feared.

"And stop that infernal humming."

Jacotte turned to make clear the source of the noise—Christophe, behind her.

The priest approached him. "That's you?"

Christophe said nothing.

"I know about you and your transhumance."

The boy raised his hands in self-defense. Father Anthonie, already moving on to another, had been confused by the word as well. More than once in his reading he was sent to his dictionary. Transhumance, he was relieved to learn, was not a sexual practice of the ancients, but a shepherd's long-distance migration to fresh pasture—like the journey of this young devil sitting behind Jacotte, this Christophe from south of the mountains.

It was the old custom of sister villages, north and south, to offer social comfort to visiting herders. Just so, the Jauffre family had thrown another tick in their barn and allowed Christophe the occasional hour of sheltered rest, sharing the loft with Roland. As if the local boy needed any more encouragement in his descent.

Jacotte had been out walking for peace of mind, she'd told the father, and thus had been first to see Christophe coming toward Gontrin, bruised and limping. She offered him water and a bit of conversation. No more than was due him. She couldn't deny she'd seen him. How could you miss a flock of two thousand? It was like a fluffy white cloud stuck to the hillside, shifting this way and that, plus the bleating.

Jacotte had admitted she gave Christophe her name straightaway, not the act of a faithful wife. And when he said these were the Spanish lord's sheep, that he had been beaten by rival shepherds, she passed on his sorry condition to the farmer Jauffre, who went out looking for the boy himself to offer his protection, bread, and shelter. Soon enough Christophe was well and able, and grazing in Gontrin, even flirting with the child, Rixende.

All this was on the father's mind as he moved down the aisle.

"One thing leads to another," he said.

The church was warming with the day. His undergarments were soaking as he stared into the frightened eyes of yet another girl, Adelh Faurée, whom he believed had lost her honor to the boy fidgeting beside her. The curé would not give up his gaze, and Adelh asked in confusion, "Leads to once upon a time?"

"Be quiet," he said, moving. "Pay attention. In a connubium there are responsibilities."

He was flustered again, confused by what he had said. He hadn't meant to use this other word from his reading—*connubium*. He took it to mean the community in all its sexual potential. He disliked the academic presumption of it, the implication of inevitability, of fornications sprinkled outside the marriage beds. He preferred to think of a population sufficient to all his flock's legitimate needs, with no cause to wander, but some of his people had strayed to the valley.

"Never mind," Father Anthonie began again. "Eight hundred years ago . . . " He described for them the woman from his reading, the woman of Gontrin named Beatrice who, like Jacotte, had gone alone down the meadows to the north. Like Jacotte, she was a woman past thirty with a long grievance against her village. Her husband left home one morning and never returned.

His point taken, he watched his audience shift in their seats, turning toward Jacotte. Cecil bobbed along in front. There was no way to ignore him.

"Sit still, won't you!"

But Cecil was soon at it again, as if a higher authority insisted he affirm and coax the message along.

"Beatrice had a single black braid," the father said, "she was a pretty woman but for a cleft lip that forced her either to smile or seem to be sneering."

He saw Jacotte reach back to pull her long dark braid through her fist. She brushed her fingers over her lips, as if assuring herself that no change had come over her face. Why, Father Anthonie reasoned, shouldn't he give fictitious flesh and personality to Beatrice if it would produce a useful inquiry?

Like everyone else who walked away from Gontrin, he told them, Beatrice had her journey interrupted by a shepherd. The white hillside in front of her moved this way and that. She was surrounded by moiling wool, as far as she could see. And fenced by animals, she came face to face with a stranger. The man was grizzled, and had not had human company for weeks, unshaven, smelly as a urine pit, and his first word to her was "Baaaah."

The Boret child, Rixende, began to laugh.

"This is not funny!"

Father Anthonie saw her curl her lip again, and tighten her jaw against him. "Are you ready to listen now?" he asked.

He raised his eyes heavenward for strength against the aggravation, for inspiration, and when he began again, his story came to him as easily as if he were reading from the holy text, a sign to him that he was on the right path. He surprised himself with detail far beyond the scholar's descriptions. Nothing seemed out of the way, even when he told them Beatrice had remarked on the man's horrid smell. And how the shepherd had replied, "dirty outside, holy within," before parting his tangled hair and revealing a red torture on his scalp.

"Did she flee from this man with the infested head?" the Curé asked.

"But of course."

It was Adelh Faurée behind him. The curé spun around.

No! No! No! He poured scorn on her mistake, waving his finger.

No, he said. When loneliness is stronger than faith, repulsiveness may take a full turn and become a charm.

Jacotte Pons was hiding her face behind her hands as he went back to his story, explaining how Beatrice had told the man her name, and was soon picking the lice from his head, squashing them, one by one, between her thumbnails.

And one thing led to another, he said, bowing sorrowfully to the altar, crossing himself, preparing them all for worse.

There was a sudden commotion, two arms thrown up.

"I don't use my thumbnails," Jacotte burst out. "There wasn't a louse on Christophe's head, anyway." She swung around to face the Spaniard. "A few nits perhaps. Any decent woman would have done the same."

Father Anthonie raised his own arms for peace in the chapel, but his eye, caught in the blue beam from Saint Gontrin's window, was twinkling in satisfaction at her discomfort.

This is old history I'm telling you, he said. Though he knew that none of them, not his housekeeper, and least of all Jacotte, was fooled by the eight-hundred-year-old scrim he had pulled down over his story—all but fully transparent—and Roland Malet was moving forward not to miss what the curé might reveal next.

Then his head was in her lap, Father Anthonie said. A thorough job would take, what would you say, an hour?

"Mother does Monsieur Jauffre in twenty minutes."

It was Adelh again, who could not bite her tongue, only trying to be helpful.

Father Anthonie looked to heaven again.

One hour, he repeated. Time for the man's cajoling to bring Beatrice to tattle on every Cathar in the village.

Jacotte stood this time to defend herself. "Christophe asked me the price of a piglet in the village, and if I would keep one for him till the fall. I betrayed no one."

For confirmation she turned again to the young Spaniard, who was suddenly uncomfortable in the church, dumb in the sight of Heaven and the curé.

"I could not, I told him," Jacotte said, "because I was on my way to the city, and might not be coming back."

"Yes, but here you sit in Gontrin," the curé said. Pleased with this progress, he walked to the first step of the altar. With his back to them, he returned to the past. Beatrice, he explained, was getting used to the foul smell of her shepherd. What should have been repulsive became intoxicating. The fingers she ran through his hair were no longer in search of lice.

Malet was making a final move forward to a seat just behind Adelh Faurée, who glared at him. Her boyfriend made the rudest gesture with his whole arm. Father Anthonie crossed himself.

"You aren't paying attention," he said. "Listen!" He explained how Beatrice told the shepherd her husband had been one of the Cathars, who believed the end of the world would not be such a bad thing. With the departure of human souls, Satan would be left all alone. It was part of their creed, the curé said, and not so complicated. Since they believed all things were determined before they happened, it was nearly impossible to sin. A thief was only an evil spirit doing what it must.

And do you see what that led to? he asked. There was silence in the church.

"The men could take pleasure with any willing partner," he said, "with no fear of punishment. All joy was innocent. One thing led to another."

He had their full attention now. Cecil's head was still at last, and Jacotte sat like a piece of red-veined marble, blushing in all her parts. He lowered his voice.

"The shepherd touched Beatrice's lips," he said, "and told her that her mouth was beautiful, and to let it speak the truth. Had she killed her husband?

"Yes, she told him. He held her arm and would not let go. She gave in. Their positions were reversed; her head was cradled between his thighs. To her, the filthy hands and face were only sun-bronzed now. Whether the stench came from the sheep dung on his oily trousers or, God forbid, his own unwashed fundament, the fetid air over his lap was driving her to madness.

"The shepherd asked Beatrice where her husband was."

Jacotte stood up and pushed her way out of her pew.

"Christophe did not smell!" she yelled. "Someone beat him near to death. He couldn't walk. As for my husband, his whereabouts are his own business."

She was lashing out at all of them, and Jauffre's daughter accused her.

"You were in my father's barn Friday night. You walked out with the Spaniard and Roland. Everyone saw you."

Father Anthonie, guiding Jacotte back into her pew, was explaining how the shepherd loosened Beatrice's tongue. How it took no wine, only the prospect of flesh and flesh.

He saw Jacotte's fury, her quivering lips forming the words "pig" and then "bastard."

"But you did," Rixende called from across the aisle, looking straight at her. "You went into the barn with both of them, and they were singing the dirty song when they walked out."

They were turning on Jacotte like a pack of dogs, and Adelh's young man woke to the moment with a helpful enthusiasm. "She was buttering the whole village with it."

Father Anthonie beat his hand against the end of a pew and the noise rattled through the nave like a kettledrum.

"That's disgusting!" he said. "How the devil would you know, anyway? Shut up, won't you? Shut up, all of you!"

They didn't see that he wasn't concerned now with their petty dalliances, or even their fornications. This was an inquiry into something worse. He slid back into the story of Beatrice.

"The shepherd had asked again, where was her husband? and she told him, maybe right there in the meadow, looking for her. If you were a Cathar, you could believe his soul was searching the earth for a seeded womb, looking for a fetus to inhabit.

"How had she killed him? the shepherd wanted to know."

Jacotte's voice rang out. "Take your smelly story somewhere else. If you want to know where my husband is, why don't you ask your housekeeper?"

With that Cecil was up and gone, out of the church. They were all laughing. The father could only go on. "Beatrice gave the shepherd names of the heretics," he said, "and then it was all turned around on her. He was no shepherd after all, but an agent of the Inquisition."

"Your own housekeeper," Jacotte repeated.

Adelh, trying to help the curé past his confusion, said, "where they click on the Google."

Jacotte was trying to leave the church. He moved in front of her, blocking the way. Enraged, she struck at him with both hands. Malet and the Spaniard restrained her.

"Cliquez?" she yelled at him. "Cliquez? Never mind the cliquez!" She was bent over, sobbing, barely able to say, "Are you satisfied?"

"Stay where you are!" he said.

They disobeyed; even the young Rixende was walking out. They were looking balefully at him as they withdrew, making him the culprit now, offering Jacotte their hands of support. She had the Jauffre girl in front, pushing past him, and Rixende at her elbow. The young men followed, respectfully behind, saying nothing.

There was no time for him to explain Beatrice's reward for her honesty, how agents of the Inquisition had returned to her village to gather the accused in a fell swoop. Every man and woman over twelve had been burned alive. It was the only way, their bishop had said, to rid the village of the general contagion. If there were mistakes, God could sort them out later.

The curé walked alone into his village, regretting his presumption. He thought he understood now. There was a café in Prades where computers could be used for a fee. The missing Pons was there, squandering his money. Back in the rectory, the father found a note from Cecil, along with his dinner cooling on the kitchen table. A message had come from the bishop in Carcassonne. He was coming midweek to discuss the trouble in the district.

PART TWO

Retribution

The curé would be ready this time. Never mind the situation in Gontrin. The bishop might be surprised to learn that the Devil was traveling through all French air. There was a new contagion, this one showering down from satellites and over wires, shocking pictures that could warp a settled life and take a man from his home. Father Anthonie went to bed thinking he might have plumbed to the base of this modern error.

By morning his duty was clearer to him. He was in the village taxi on his way to Prades to fetch Pons home before the bishop arrived in Gontrin on Wednesday. It wouldn't take a threat of excommunication to turn such a simple man around. The father had the taxi to himself and could relax on the journey. He removed his collar to arrive in the valley as a spy.

In the town they passed a church larger than his own, and drove through a respectable neighborhood, but at the dark edges of the place, they turned into a street where a lone woman stood on the corner in pants shiny as polished leather. As they slowed and turned in front of her, she stepped into the street to stop them. The driver warned her out of the way with his horn. As they went past, she spat.

"A live one," the driver said.

Best to explain nothing, the father thought. On the way home, with Pons in tow, it could be cleared up. Cecil might even make himself useful, explain exactly what the man had been doing with the computer in Prades. At the end of the same street they came to the place, its name painted on the glass front: Internet Café; and beneath that, *Escalier à Paradis*, the Stairway to Heaven. Drawn blinds covered the window.

Inside, Father Anthonie faced a stairway and a sign on the wall, a hand and finger pointing upward. To the side was a doorway into the café. There were six small screens with keyboards along two walls of the room, and in the rear behind a bar, coffee machines on one side, liquor bottles on the other. Several young men and a woman were seated at the computers. He was without his glasses but he could see the white text tumbling down the dark screens, as their fingers moved over the keys. This would be the sending and receipt of the electric mail, he supposed. His man was nowhere to be seen. The father asked at the business counter for their customer Pons.

"No names here. We didn't ask yours, eh?"

Not knowing how to order, he pointed at the machine frothing milk. A cappuccino, well sugared, quickened his mind, and even in this room where he supposed the Devil might arrive in an electric instant, a euphoria of good intentions came over him. He felt certain of delivering his man home to Gontrin.

Two hours later, the father was still there. A newspaper read twice over was no longer credible cover for his watchful waiting. He ordered another cappuccino. He'd seen nothing untoward on the screens, only the alphabet falling all around the room, tier after tier of letters. He studied the smiles and grimaces, the silent concentration of the operators. New people came and went. Just at dusk, with all the positions filled, there was a frenzy of communication. The chirping of the

machines reminded him of pigeons pecking at the cobblestones in the park at Carcassonne, the calming
sound before his last audience with the bishop.

He'd brought no travel kit, but could make do. He ordered a room.

"For the whole night?"

"Yes, of course," the priest said. Though the fee was
beyond reason, it was the price of perseverance, and it
wasn't his money after all, but the church's.

"We have four of them," he was told. "Would you
care for a look?"

That wouldn't be necessary. "But quiet." He insisted
on that.

"They're all quiet," he was told. "You won't hear a
peep. Dark or light?"

"Oh, it must be dark," he said. "And perhaps in the
rear."

There was sudden laughter among the men drinking
at the bar behind him. He felt pushed into an old man's
part again, aware of joking at his expense. A third coffee brought on his palpitations, and he went carefully,
unsteadily, into the street.

Around the corner and two blocks away he found a
restaurant where he sat for calf's liver and fried potatoes. An hour later, revived, he returned to the café.
The scene had changed. A grim woman was walking
back and forth at the doorway with a sign that read

FERMEZ L'ABOMINATION! She called "Shame!" as he walked past. Someone raised a camera and took his picture. The light flashing in his face didn't worry him; rather it gave a hint of celebrity to his mission.

Inside, the room was filled with tobacco smoke. The only light came from a bulb hanging from the ceiling, and the glow of the computer screens. Taking the part of a regular, he pulled his stool closer to the bar and ordered a beer, ready to join whatever conversation came his way, waiting for the right moment to inquire again about Pons. No sign of the man, but the curé's relaxed approach brought immediate fellowship. From the next stool came a friendly finger in the rib, and whispering.

"Better than a tongue in your ear and a lot of silly squawking, eh?"

The man was staring straight ahead, honoring anonymity, even as he shared this strange confidence. Perhaps if the father stayed long enough he'd begin to understand the masculine language used here in the Internet Café. He wished he had something sympathetic, something modern to say to the gentleman, but was afraid he'd set off another fit of laughter.

The man spoke again, directly to his own image in the mirror behind the bar.

"The one at the end, he likes the flaxen. You favor the Dinge, eh?" He felt the finger in his ribs again. "Each to his own." Looking at his watch, the man went on, "Just off nine . . . "

Father Anthonie ordered a second beer, and risked a question. "Waiting to send a letter, are you? Waiting for inspiration?" With this he forfeited his privacy. The gentleman swiveled to explore his face.

Anxious to explain himself, the father forgot his lay disguise. "Of course the church pays for my night here. I couldn't afford it."

The man looked at him as at a liar or an imbecile, got up from his stool, and walked to the end of the bar to take up with someone else. They were staring back at him as another mysterious cheer went up in the room. His glass was being filled again just as he was tapped on the shoulder and told his room was ready. He was grateful for the excuse to retire.

Number Four was not in the rear as he'd requested but in the front of the building. Entering the room, he could not credit the scene. In the candlelit haze a black woman knelt, naked on the bed, her underparts smooth and swollen, facing him in the doorway.

"Get out!" he said.

She made no reply, didn't move a muscle.

He took another step into the room, then a short one backward, the way he might approach an animal that could be dangerous. Still nothing. To the father, who had not seen a mature naked woman since childhood glimpses of his own mother, it was a remarkable thing. Her chocolate skin glistened, anointed head to toe with some lotion. Her limbs were toned to shapeliness beyond reality, unblemished. It was an immediate wonder to him that any woman would spend such perfection in this self-abasement.

He considered a homily, but thought better of it. He thought of Henri Pons. What man in his congregation wouldn't have been lured if this extraordinary temptation fell, unbidden and with no witness to his weakness, into his bed? He was aware of his own moment of doubt and the sensation in his groin that had even been ruled out of his dreams.

"Get out!" he said again, louder.

She ignored him. He came closer and stood beside her. In his beer muddle, her eyes seemed expressionless, her lips locked in a round pout. If she thought he was going to let her stay here, she was dealing with the wrong customer. Her body, behind the candlelight, threw a grotesque silhouette, huge melon shapes, against the room's stained walls. Agape at the catatonic performance, he poked her thigh. The skin was cold and lifeless, smooth and impermeable. His finger left a dimple that took a moment to recover. He pushed again, harder, and the brazen lady toppled onto her side, arms and legs sticking forward in the same kneeling position, like a doll's limbs waiting to be readjusted.

He backed out of the room, calling for help. And there was his own man Cecil in front of him. Even in this dim light and without his glasses there was no mistaking the face. He was coming down the hall carrying a woman barely covered in a sheer gown, revealing an outline as lovely as it was obscene. But for her pale skin and long blond hair, she was the very image of the lady in his room. Lifeless as a sack of grain, drunk to stupefaction he supposed, and bent nearly double over Cecil's shoulder, arms and legs hanging straight down. More curious, her mouth was open in that same pleading circle, as if formed in the same mold.

It didn't seem cowardly at the moment, more like turning his back on depravity, as he passed them in the hallway without a word, walked down the steps and out of the building. The cool night air began to sober him as he went down the street in search of another taxi. In his brief inebriation, the women had seemed no more than mannequins. The Negress in his room, dead to the world before he ever spoke to her, or touched her. Beyond help. There might be a chance to get the whole story from Cecil before he let the man go.

At the rectory cottage Father Anthonie was not sure where to begin in preparing himself for the bishop's visit. Cecil had returned to Gontrin as if nothing had happened. He was whistling through a day's chores, rushing to be done and away again, and diffident as ever in the face of his curé's question, "What's going on in Prades, Cecil? Where is Pons?"

"If you saw nothing, I saw nothing."

Stunned by the impudence, Father Anthonie retreated to his books to ponder. Cecil seemed to think they were on equal moral footing, in a standoff. Instead of immediate dismissal he thought it prudent to let the man come to him with his confession and promise of reform. It took forbearance, but that might be the best way with a personality like Cecil's; let the guilt mature. Besides, it would be good to have someone else pour the extra glass of sherry for the bishop. Cecil would show contrition or be gone by the end of the week.

As the day passed Father Anthonie became less sure of himself, and less sure of what had happened in Prades, of what he had touched in the candlelight. And when the bishop arrived, the curé found himself jumping awkwardly to the middle of his story. "Perhaps just a prurient decoration . . . for casual amusement . . . of course, I had no idea . . . "

The bishop gave him plenty of room. He spoke of the quality of wine the church was receiving, and enlisted Father Anthonie in a campaign to embarrass the vineyards. If they were going to tithe in kind, they ought not to foist an inferior vintage on this diocese "as if we were still harboring heretics."

That was all it took to launch the father again.

"Heretics . . . "

He explained the tangled path that led from Beatrice, to Jacotte, into the Internet Café, and up the Stairway to Heaven.

The bishop took one of the father's hands between his own as a parent might take a child's while turning his head away from shame. "You know, Anthonie. We have to keep step with the gadgets. And remember, there's no filth in the word, only in the mind."

The curé was explaining the relevance of Beatrice to the disappearance of Henri Pons. The bishop let him go on, but seemed to be listening to another voice, responding to another story, one less fraught and more reliable. Without summons, Cecil poured his second sherry. "You have a fine man, here," the bishop said. And with a flourish of largesse he told the curé he was safe in his job for the time being.

Later that week the father saw Henri Pons in the bakery, head bowed to Jacotte as she overruled his order of a pastry. The man was not dead and stuffed in a closet; he was home in family harness. But Pons' Sunday confession might as well have been an outright lie. His only regret after his week in Prades was for a single blasphemy and a failure to pray. Why should the father assign an act of contrition to this pitiful portion of truth? There'd come a time when conscience would overtake Pons, just as it would overtake Cecil. The father could wait.

Still, he had not fired Cecil, who said the frequent travel to Prades was exhausting, that he would quit there as soon as he found another job. But *his* last effort in the confessional was a disappointment, too. There was no confession; rather, a profession of solidarity.

"I don't just want to work for you, Father," he whispered, "I want to be a friend, share the secret."

"Of course you can be a friend! But this is no place for gossip! We have no secrets."

"But yes, we have one." There was no malice in Cecil's response, no warning. He hesitated as he explained. "The manager says he's sorry for our mistake. . . . Of course, you didn't want the black. He says you may use the back door."

Father Anthonie dismissed him from the booth with only the slightest penalty, a dozen beads. Back in the parsonage he told Cecil, "You can't work here anymore."

Cecil was looking at the floor, responding to the hearthstones. "The fireplace is clean. And I've changed the sheets. Your dinner is ready. I can't be here tomorrow."

"I'm firing you, Cecil. Do you understand?"

The following Sunday there were only a handful of people at his service, but Cecil was there, bobbing along with the father's voice through the whole thing, and the dependable Adelh Faurée, who afterward said it was too disgusting, what was happening in Prades. Though not to worry, she didn't believe it about the curé. He hurried away from her and several others of his faithful.

Midweek he returned from a walk through the village and found Cecil back in the parsonage.

"What are you doing?"

Cecil nodded at the rag in his hand.

"Go!" Father Anthonie told him. "Get out!"

"When I'm finished."

"You won't be paid."

This didn't seem to matter. The father turned away, again retreating to the side room, to his books. He took down the parish log and wrote.

> Cecil came back today in the purple shirt. How do you fire a man in a village where there are no constables and no locks on the doors? He insists on working here. I suppose I should count that in his favor. The parish is squabbling over me. Monsieur Faurée supports me, but the farmer Jauffre is writing a letter to the bishop. I was not myself in Prades. Palpitations. It's an appalling slavery there.

With this entry, he made his innocence in the thing a matter of record in his own handwriting. A few were blessing him for his patience with Cecil, but others had no more use for his preaching. It took the father only a week more to break the stubborn Cecil, who was offering servility in return for the respectability of employment in the rectory. Hurt by the father's refusal to direct his chores, or even speak to him, the spirit went out of him. In the end, when he understood the curé had meant what he said, there would be no pay for the work, he became abusive.

"No one's coming to your church. They won't tell you anything."

Father Anthonie was reminded of the Faurée girl's last confession, which had been more a tutorial for him than her.

"They use them," she said.

"Use them?"

"Use!"

Adelh was impatient, trying to tell him what he could have seen for himself if he'd gone to Prades with the imagination or curiosity of an ordinary man.

With his congregation dwindling, he had second thoughts about Cecil. Perhaps a visit and a more complete explanation would soften the village heart. He strolled toward the low quarter of Gontrin.

Approaching Cecil's cottage, its stucco chipped and cracking and mortar crumbling from the stones beneath, he saw the power and phone lines from a distant pole, drooping together almost to head level in the yard before rising again to their attachment under the eave. More astonishing was the computer itself, its screen alight with a pattern of revolving planets, and the keyboard on an ancient oak table, the first things you saw as you ducked through the doorway.

A glance took in the other furnishings—two chairs, a knife, fork, and spoon wedged between nails over a dry sink, a small frying pan, gray saucepan, two plates and a cup held behind a strip of wood on another wall, and a metal cot with bare tick and single blanket, on which Cecil lay with his back to the room.

"What do you want?" he asked, shifting only his head in the curé's direction.

"I want you to show me how it works," the father said, pointing to the computer.

"I don't have to show you anything."

"Of course not," he said, stooping to back out as he'd entered.

"No. Come in here." Cecil, taking a sudden interest in the visit, roused himself and took a chair at the table. "Sit," he said.

At the touch of a button the turning planets gave way to a clear screen. Type moved out in a line as Cecil punched the keys, and his lips moved over the letters: *www.virtual doll/*

The screen turned black and was framed with red curtains. Another click and the title was translated: *Poupée Real.*

"There you are, Monsieur Le Curé. You're in the doll house again."

Women appeared on the screen, exactly like those he'd seen at the Internet Café, identically shaped sisters, black, Asian, caucasian; every one naked and pouting. His eyes skipped along in the text beneath the pictures. All he could think to say was, "Turn it off. How do you afford this?"

The Internet Café paid, he said. "They know I have curious visitors."

Home, he was shamed again by where he'd been. Cecil had drawn him into the hidden room in America with only the electronic address; the place where they came from, the plastic dolls hollowed both here and there for service. For fifteen thousand francs you could have one flown across the ocean, delivered to your door. The Café had four of them, locked away in a closet until the moon rose on this strange temptation. If these women had arrived on the slopes of the Pyrenees, had they come to the rest of France as well? His mind slipped backward over his nation's defense against the migrants. The Immigration Service? Customs? The National Health?

The father was subdued going about his duties that fall, nursing his humiliation, anticipating the bishop's return for a midwinter inspection of the Gontrin parish. Resigned to his disgrace, he waited to be told he would lose his vestments to a new curé. In the meantime someone tried to burn down the Internet Café in Prades. How would the stench of synthetic women burning compare to the flesh at the stake eight hundred years earlier?

Father Anthonie prepared no sermon for the bishop's return, leaving the problem to its moment, knowing the danger he could be to himself. The moment came and there was only his injured innocence to inform his argument.

Left behind, was he? No one was left behind. The web that concerned him was not made of electrons squirting filthy pictures or business correspondence or *billets-doux* across the planet. It was a pattern woven, destroyed, and rewoven as by a tireless spider, the universal conscience, the same thread in which all history was caught—Beatrice, who tattled on her village; Jacotte, who defied her own, the careless young of Gontrin; himself; and his patronizing bishop.

"No one is left behind," he shouted into his church, looking the bishop in the eye. Few, if any, understood because it left all preface to the imagination. All of us, he said, still looking directly at the bishop.

The bishop stared straight back at him. He had nothing to say after the service. His letter arrived before the next Sunday. "Your retirement is well-earned," he said. The diocese would provide for the curé, but modestly, in a cottage in the lower village without electricity or phone. "I think you know the surplice and undervestments must convey, and should be sent down to Carcassonne for dry cleaning."

Among the majority in the community there was sadness and shame for their part in his fall. It would be a trial, breaking in a new man, getting him used to their eccentricities and failings. Father Anthonie walked among them, nodding this way and that at any gesture of respect. Stripped of religious office there was a new ease in his voice, and a gentler allowance for the backsliders.

As seasons passed he began to be taken for a village wise man, a raconteur in the bar, where his rambling over faith and heresy met with tolerance, and sometimes veneration, which he knew derived more from a lazy ignorance than his own acumen. Neither civil authority nor the church had stamped out the disorder in Prades.

They were all of them infected with the knowledge of it, the soulless infestation. Without a pulpit, he spoke into the mirror behind the bar like a stranger in the Internet Café. As if Cecil were not sitting there right beside him, comfortable in dissent, the excommunicated beside the defrocked, throwing Father Anthonie's own words back at the glass.

"Where everything is forbidden, everything is allowed. Otherwise, how could we breathe?" Yet he was mindful of the waste, of some lost soul wandering in the valley, perhaps from an earlier century, searching for a new fetus to inhabit and erring into a womb of plastic, facing a barren eternity.

She'd already laid her scent,
commercially available pheromones
that hung in the stacks like
a lusty dew.

4

The Ricus Adams

"Come in, for God's sake, if you're coming!"

Lisa, sitting behind the sales counter, raised her head from a stale volume of no particular interest to her, though surely of value to someone.

"Come on, then, silly twit," she said, "make up your mind."

The sleek woman, visible through the glass, was pacing back and forth as if unable to decide whether entry were worth her while.

She caught Lisa's eye through the window and waved.

Lisa slapped down the dull book, went to the door, and cheery as a sparrow, welcomed Margot D'Espere into The Endless Shelf.

Lisa Raimond had come into the book business the same way she played gin, a bit of a fool for her own advice: "Pick up the whole pile. Things you want are hiding there." As if multiple discards were bound to yield a net gain.

Her father had given her the building, the shell of his former dry cleaning business, with a grudging generosity and a warning that it was all she had coming from him. He retired, moved to New England, and would not reconcile himself to her new career.

Lisa had disappointed him in every way, shilly-shallying through school and college, through perfunctory jobs and a line of gentleman friends, all chosen to fail, certain to fail, in the face of her refusal to be provided for. It was not just cussed, he said, but stubborn and futile, a path to the bitterest sort of self-reliance, independence nourished by failures.

"And now this," he said, a venture into the unlikeliest of businesses, used book sales. Lucky for her, he wasn't around to see for himself, the way she was gathering her stock. At estate sales her rule was, Take it all. She was a snob about paperbacks; trashed them on sight. She had no special taste for American authors, but called herself "a bit of a fool" for the English.

Actually some respectable private libraries were moved intact into the former dry cleaning place in the Virginia village where she hung her sign, THE ENDLESS SHELF. Not endless, though the back room, thirty feet wide and fifty deep, held a mile of gray metal racks bought at surplus. And Lisa had begun to pad out her mile with the leftovers of book fairs and yard sales.

It hadn't yet come home to her that a vast collection of commonplace editions might be stultifying, or that doors open to the public would oblige her to treat the pathologies of stray seekers of book talk, company, and even affection. Margot D'Espere, for example, who said she was looking for anything at all on the history of dental medicine, cuing herself for "You were so wise not to let them close that space between your teeth."

Tall and trim, with eyes that raked, Margot lowered herself to Lisa, tilting backward from knees and waist, her head cocked and waiting.

"Or do you have something about butterflies finding their way back to a tree in Brazil?"

No, Lisa had nothing like that. Perhaps it had been in a magazine.

"Probably," Margot allowed. "But it's a nice idea. When I think of all the people who know my address and can't find my door anymore."

She was holding a checkbook at the ready, as if some sign of tolerance must be shown before it could be opened. Lately, she said, the antiquarian dealers had not been kind. Locking up, or disappearing when she arrived. One by one, the trade was shutting her out.

"They'll never touch my father's books," she assured Lisa.

"Ummm," was all the encouragement Margot needed.

Self began to flow from her as if under pressure behind an opened tap, her mouth, otherwise not unat-
tractive, wide and heavy lipped. No use Lisa turning
her back on it; bio was squirting out regardless.

"Start with my parents. Still clinging to Victorian
remnants."

She had a sister who was committed from time to
time for confusing herself with a Belgian queen and a
brother who spent much of a day washing his hands.
Her own weakness, she confessed, was a bookshop. "I
could spend all day."

Lisa had no time for a family of exotics. She was
moving toward the back room, Margot in pursuit with
her pathetic vita. There was high school cheating, expulsion from college, a marriage undermined by a therapist whose advice—self-actualization—was embraced
by an all too eager husband. Now she was back in her
parents' house.

"Time enough for reading. I suppose you keep the
erotica out of sight."

Teeth and butterflies the least of her interests, as it
turned out. At the first sign of Lisa's aversion, Margot
shifted into a lower conversational gear.

"Imagine us at the dinner table. My father just in
from his library, fingers sticky from pasting his *ex libris*
label in another prize volume. My mother tells him I've
refused to do my lessons again. For my punishment we
have to watch, course by course, as Daddy refuses to
eat his dinner."

As she spoke, Margot was moving further back into the stacks, drawn to provocative dust jackets and titles that slanted south into venereal territory. Love manuals through history, fiction that massaged, biography that cross-dressed, and all collectible.

After the first week of curious browsing, the traffic in Lisa's new store fell to a trickle. A hand resting against the front glass might pass for a morning's only promise. But Margot became a regular. Quite shameless, the way she came back and back to go finger walking over the mile of spines for anything that might tease a libido, and to pass along to Lisa more family drama.

Margot's book-collecting father, Christophe D'Espere, first presented as a master of passive offense, was no longer a threat, but mute and immobile. "Three strokes and you're out," Margot explained. "He's in a wheelchair."

Lisa was not being quite honest when she wrote to tell her own father.

I've taken on someone as a sort of project. Her name is Margot D'Espere. Margot of Hope if you're French. Margot the Hopeless to the American ear and to all outward appearances.

An obvious vamp, but I'm counting on the French translation.

She didn't say the woman often filled an empty and anxious silence in the shop. And Margot's collecting went on. Week by week, searching for yet another book from Lisa's shelves to answer a warm yearning or give it license. She was always promising "my father's books when the time comes."

By the spring Lisa had resigned herself to losses, probably for the first year or two. Closing the shop for a week, she went for a regional tour of other dealers, to have a look-see at how they managed. And all of them seemed to be hiding something, covetous even of the musty air that barely moved through their closely watched shelves.

It seemed a little insane the way they lived, all on the lookout for some grail—for some volume that could quicken their pulses and make them fools. Something so rare it was barely attainable, and which, if it ever came their way, would be grabbed and never released. The quirk that made their lesser treasures saleable.

"What are you after?" they all wanted to know.

In fact Lisa was surprised to learn how much the area's antiquarians already knew about her. Their scouts had been through her shop soon after its opening. It was the Annapolis bookman O'Connor who brought her up short.

"You've gone about it all wrong," he said. "You need a dumpster at the back door for most of that trash. And don't waste your day with shiftless neurotics."

She'd only asked O'Connor for advice. Instead he attacked her. "Your store isn't needed. You haven't a clue."

Hopkins in Kensington was more amiable. "It's not too late for you. But you'll need a specialty." He did

British military history with a side in ocean liner memorabilia. Deck plans, passenger lists, and the like. His shop, as so many others, imposed a fussy silence broken every hour or two by a tinkling over the door. Always the air of erudition suffering the insult of commerce. His prices made her flinch.

Hopkins sent her on to Blue-Gray in Takoma Park, to the gnarly Watts, who sat under stacks of Civil War history high enough to topple, defending his garrison, as afraid as his General McClellan that someone might get the better of him. He asked if she'd met Lucas, the decorator.

"Lucas buys anything in leather or half leather," Hopkins explained. "He'll be around."

Lisa was directed to Colophon in Alexandria, where Mabel Winton fussed over collectible American fiction with the odd walk-in. Here Lisa was lectured again.

"You can't just be a warehouse . . . Not convinced yet? Talk to Caulkins. He's made a small fortune."

Did she have the address wrong? Caulkins came to the door of his residence in robe and slippers at noon, holding together the balsa skeleton of a model plane, a tube of glue in his teeth. Not a shelf in sight. At the moment, he had only seven books tucked away in cupboards and closets.

"I'll tell you what I tell them all," he said. "Be an opportunist. Otherwise people use you as their trash man. And remember, if they don't know what they have, they don't deserve to know. Screw 'em!"

"Gordon's in Fairfax does it my way," Lisa argued. "They have a huge collection with no order to it. People rummaging everywhere."

"That's all theater," Caulkins said. "Don't be fooled. They have a ferret."

Lisa returned from her tour chastened and wiser. The real dealers were perched around the city ready to swoop on single prey, a client's coveted title or the odd literary trinket of their own eccentric yearning. When the doors of the Vassar Book Sale swung open they were there in a flock. And a few moments later the tables were picked clean of the good stuff. Hovering over estate sales, hoping to snatch the lean and leave the fat. They reminded her of Pritchett's English antique men, cliquish in their furtive questing. All of them experts tolerating the ignorance of customers with a show of patience. She never connected her suspicion of the trade with its improbable foundation, that a book, prime symbol of the humanitarian instinct, might swell in value after publication.

As the weeks passed Lisa began to understand what the veteran bookmen wanted from her—reciprocal privilege within their order, and arm's length to the public. The common customer's innocence was their livelihood. Her naïvete was an inconvenience to all of them.

At summer's end, when Lisa was considering closing her doors for good, a stranger appeared in the shop. Disheveled and intense, he came in the back door as if drawn to the scent of the books themselves. Without introducing himself he examined inventory.

"Yes, you want a better home, don't you."

He was patting a spine, and seemed to be speaking not to her but a pet.

Not your home, Lisa guessed; his rumpled clothes had the look of twenty-four-hour habitat. A book held high in front of him couldn't conceal a flush of self-consciousness rising in red bloom across his soft, childish face. He spoke gently to another book, then another. In short order he carried his selection of three to the front.

He thought each of them could be placed quite easily. But he wasn't buying any of them himself.

"This one," he said, "keep it close to you."

"Really?" she asked. "What would it bring?"

The color drained back into his neck. He looked shocked, as if she'd asked the price of a child, and he ambled back through the stacks and out the same door he'd come in, leaving her free to phone Annapolis.

"It's by Flan O'Brien," she told O'Connor. "*At Swim Two Birds.*"

She could hear his quickened breath as he leafed through one of his guides. "London?" he asked. "Nineteen thirty-nine?"

"Yes. Yes."

"Black cloth?"

"Yes."

"Hold on to it. I'll pick it up."

By week's end it was sold for three thousand, and the stranger came back to introduce himself as David Seaton. Through the front door this time. He was asking Lisa for a job.

"Minimum wage," he pleaded. "I'd just like to spend more time with your collection."

As if her motley of titles deserved a steady, critical attention.

"You can't live on that. There's nothing special here."

"I can, and there is," he said. "You'll see. The only thing is, I have to take exercise three times a week. For this." He made a vague pass across his chest.

"Family?"

There was no self pity in his answer. "My only relatives are books."

His reference was a note from the Past Pleasures shop in Charleston.

> David Seaton worked here several months. Then he left. We are satisfied.

"It's supposed to make you laugh," he said.

She'd failed another test. He retreated to the back to wait for her answer.

"Yes"—but only so long as he proved himself valuable.

He started the next day. Hadn't been there an hour before Margot D'Espere began to work him over in the stacks.

"There's a biography of Custer here somewhere. Have you seen it?"

No, he hadn't.

"Yes, with the chapter on the trail disease. You know, too long in camp without a woman. Gonad poisoning."

He went directly to another shelf, as if the room were already arranged in a David Seaton Decimal system, and pulled down *My Life and Loves*.

"Take this instead," he told her. "Frank Harris will set you straight. Nineteenth-century gentlemen didn't spend their seed casually. They thought it left them intellectually impaired for at least a week."

Lisa imagined a petulant Margot. What with David's new control of territory where she'd already laid her scent, commercially available pheromones that hung in the stacks like a lusty dew. But Margot bent immediately to the new ear, and began her life story all over again. "Imagine my family at the dinner table . . . "

Lisa was soon counting on David's punctual arrival each morning. His diverse knowledge entertained and brightened her day. He made a nice buffer between her and Margot. She thought of his chit-chat with the needy woman as harmless comedy; he was so much Margot's intellectual superior. In his second week as her modest hireling, he came to Lisa with *Two Bird Lovers in Mexico*.

"Someone will appreciate this one," he said. With *Charles W. Beebe* printed on its cover and *Boston, 1905* inside, it brought her fifteen hundred. For David's part, it seemed they were only placing another worthy orphan. This one had been hiding on a top shelf, he said.

Quite by chance, Lisa had her ferret, but when she told Caulkins about it he quickly changed his tune.

"I've never seen a ferret yet that wouldn't bite," he told her, insinuating her business was out of control. Loiterers pawing at her stock all day, hunting aphrodisiacs. And now this conjurer of first editions. Not to be trusted.

Never mind the envious Caulkins. David Seaton had saved her shop, and she soon felt obliged to ease her rumpled man's daily struggle with life's commonplaces. Looking out for him, she was drawn quickly into the details of his minimal existence.

His book talent came with unusual deficiencies. David, who swam so easily in the sea of printed ideas, foundered on the common shore. Couldn't cook. Washed wool with everything else in hot water. Couldn't drive, or wouldn't, no sense of direction. He'd been lost once in the small grid of their own village. From a cramped apartment he could walk to work with a turn at only one corner, where he stopped at a hash house for meals.

By the second winter Lisa could take pleasure again in writing her father, this time to say her business stood on its own feet. She explained about ferrets and boasted of profit.

David is something of a miracle worker. He's adorable. I never thought knowledge could be such an aphrodisiac. Pity, I'm almost certain he's of the other persuasion. (Don't lecture.) My shop has come alive! Daddy, he knows everything. And what a nose for treasure! Last week, an original Inigo Jones drawing at the bottom of a box of silly reprints. Think of the commotion (read commission, if you like). You'd be surprised how many people don't know what's on their shelves.

Lisa was learning the delicate balance between full disclosure and taking a little profit on her clients' ignorance, while David seemed to drift above the dilemma, lighter than ethics. That week, there was his fanciful account of the Jones sketch liberated from the Duke of Devonshire by a cunning tourist. Lost, found, and onto the Endless Shelf. And that was followed by his discourse on the seventeenth-century masque as the mother of modern stagecraft.

He made so little of his learning, and Margot was captivated, too. Lisa's rich little book harlot was even making herself useful at times. The three of them, thrown together perforce, made a new and unconventional stop on the antiquarian circuit.

It was no use Lisa calling into the stacks, "Let David get back to work!" But what a spectacle they were making, with her fussing at her odd couple; Margot pouring over a volume on lactation and breast pumps, and David reading aloud from Donne's *Devotions*.

These became happy months for Lisa. She was more than fond of her bookman, pleased that he now allowed her to supplement his diet with her own pies and plastic containers of healthy soup. And he was allowing her the intimate task of his laundry, which he brought to the store each Monday morning, lights and darks separated according to her instruction.

Margot was permitted a more formal chore as chauffeur to his health club three evenings a week.

"Off again with our hussy," was his regular goodbye, letting Margot grab his arm and pull him from the shop. The farewell taken with a kiss blown to Lisa, the only kind of kissing that seemed to interest him.

Lisa always took him with her to estate appraisals, and relied on his thumbs up or down. She was sticking to her rule. Leave it, or take it all. A thousand volumes always provided cover for a prize or two. When a full collection was safely in the shop, a gilt edge would begin to glow for David's sharp eye.

There was still sniping from the other dealers. Like the slander wrapped in Mabel Winton's question, Was it true the D'Espere woman had been seen again in Hopkins' place with a flushed face and an unidentified man, the two of them hurrying out the door with a full shopping bag?

No, Lisa assured her. Margot was content and pasturing daily at The Endless Shelf under the calming influence of Mr. Seaton. But Ms. Winton's insinuations were followed a week later by a rude inquiry from Past Pleasures in Charleston.

We're told David Seaton has been with you more than a year.

Would you please inform us if, since his hire, Algren's *Somebody In Boots*, New York, 1935, or Ambler's *Dark Frontier*, London, 1936, have turned up in your shop.

yrs. very truly,

J. L. Stevey, mgr.

As near to libel, she thought, as Mr. Stevey could come. Lisa felt closer to her two rare birds now, pleased to think she was shielding them from careless insult.

She liked to imagine David as the cast-off genius of some academy he'd shamed with his uncompromising intellect. Unambitious, he had a right to his secrets and hibernation in her stacks, just as Lisa had earned her satisfaction in his peculiarity. Her early marriage and the affairs that followed might have been so many balloons filled to bursting with the breath of ordinary men.

Now she had one that might do for a lifelong entertainment, decorated with clever words, floating above the others. It was all right that he teased, a bit out of her reach, his mind playing in all directions, on chaos and order, nature's inclination to the wave form, harmonics and the ear's expectations, and across the literary ages from naughty monks to self-referencing moderns.

His hand reached into the last despised carton at a church bazaar. Out came Mr. Faulkner's *Soldier's Pay*, New York, 1926. Another first, jacket clean, no foxing, spotless.

"Impossible," Mabel Winton thought. "No, for God's sake don't mail it. I'll come by."

Mabel came for the book, toured Lisa's mile, and found it less than ordinary. She left in disbelief.

Lisa made a donation to the church where the book was found. David accepted a small raise in salary, without excitement, and got on with his reading. He was becoming quite familiar by then, calling her "a petit bourgeois" when she spent too much time with her bibliographies. It scarcely bothered her when he told customers that her stacks were walls of tripe. Even as he took Margot sporting through them again, as if they could have missed one of her easy pleasures.

When Mr. D'Espere died, Margot fell back on her dark humor. "My binary father. After the last stroke, one blink for yes, two for no." And no more mention of his books. David Seaton's coronary came a month later, without warning.

Lisa watched him collapse to the floor of the shop in midstep, coming toward her with another book, a quizzical look on his face, as if his final offering had been interrupted with bad news from an angel. The last trick of his trick heart, the problem his health club was supposed to manage.

Darker letters over a brief obituary in the community paper confirmed the impossible: David Seaton, Assistant at The Endless Shelf, Thirty-Seven.

This was all? After everything she'd told their reporter? Nothing of the grand knowledge so lightly borne that made him such a modest, witty companion. Nothing of the way her customers had adored him, trusting his casual dismissal of some piece of leather-bound trash from another century, or his enchantment with the real thing hiding in a torn paper jacket.

Lisa remembered the book falling to the floor, and pushing it aside as she threw herself on him and blew through his purple lips into a chalk-white head. It must have looked more like necrophilia than CPR. She was pulled aside by the rescue squad. They took his body, and she sat cradling the book, his last gift, in her lap.

It sat on her bed table until the second night, when waves of grief gave way to curiosity. It was an odd-shaped thing, almost square, in dark blue cloth, and on the spine, a red leather label printed in gold letters: *The Education Of Henry Adams.*

Riffling the deckled edges, back to front, she saw that much of the book had been defaced with marginalia, and verso of the title page itself inscribed in blue ink gone pale.

> Dear Ricus,
>
> I've no great confidence in this. Only 100 copies, and better perhaps there should have been ten or none. They go now to my friends and colleagues for assent, correction, or advice.
>
> Years ago didn't you stir the class in favor of my election as Orator, and just as enthusiastically criticize the oration? That same mix of favor and honesty I beg for now.
>
> Henry Adams
>
> post s. Life has been rather smaller these twenty years without Clover. You'll find no mention of her here. There are some, ignorant as dust, who will herein blame me for her loss.

The answering pencil had been wielded left and right in a wide, tendentious script.

> "This is wrong!"
>
> "No! Any road that arrives is not therefore good. Been to Concord lately?"
>
> "What gives you claim to think your 'sensitive and timid nature' has any claim on public attention?"

Lisa skipped forward through the blunt comments, her pulse suddenly driven as an adding machine by the expanding sum, the book's market value. Scrawled on an endpaper was the early reader's final comment.

> Perhaps you suffer the malady of all those lapsed Christians coddled at the University? No moral core to save them from ennui in scholarship, or from their heedless greed when they stirred themselves to commerce. Of course they can't make moral choices if they don't recognize them as such.
>
> Ricus

Lisa knew she held an association copy of the first edition, Washington, 1907, maybe for auction and a grand reward. But David floated up again, and the book fell from her weak hand among the bedclothes. She pushed it further away, shamed by her small and greedy interference in the debate of larger minds.

At the cemetery there had been an awful error, a full-size grave dug for David's urn. Under a cold January sun it was a service of every ill proportion. Inadequate tribute by the cleric, and then Margot's wailing, which made Lisa's numb silence seem puny and irrelevant. A ridiculous caterwauling with a pretense of lost affection and requited intimacy.

The next Saturday Lisa reopened at the regular hour, thinking to bury sorrow in workaday habit, but someone came in asking for the young man in her store who knew all about Frances Trollope, and she snapped at the reductive insult.

"Out! I'm closed!"

David's brain was incinerated now, all its crannies, compartments for Peloponnesian Wars, chess, pre-Raphaelites, the Angkor civilization, the Bloomsbury crowd, the Portuguese exploration, the Bauhaus, on and on. And anything of particular merit ever printed in America. All of it cremated along with his wondrous neural catalogue of the private libraries bought and sold by Lisa since he'd been with her.

She locked the shop, walked out the door, and just kept walking south, right out of her village with a linear insistence, as if she meant to put all of northern Virginia behind her. At a multilane thoroughfare she turned west, toward a mountain. Beside the highway her feet kept the rhythm of a late declaration.

"Loved him, loved him, loved him . . . "

Well, she had and she hadn't. How could anyone love such a neutered soul, fixed by the knife of his own bookish wit? Not that she hadn't tried to provoke him in the early days, and with the commonest devices— the work of an eyelash, a pout, a hand to his belt as she gave a gentle order.

Lisa looked up at a sign for Northgate Way, and knew now why she was here. It was north of nothing in particular and there was no gate, but this was the way to David's exercise parlor, his Club at Northgate. She was on her way to investigate the people who had promised David health.

A building of black stone rose over the berm. Closer, through dark glass, she saw a row of men and women in sweats and stretch suits going nowhere at different speeds. Beyond these another group climbed in vain on pedals that collapsed beneath them. And there in the line, assaulting her own indoor Annapurna, was Margot, carved into long, shameless halves by a thong leotard.

Seeing Lisa, Margot averted her eyes and stepped faster, as if defiantly on her way to the top of the world, where sorrow would not have to be shared.

Someone came out to greet her. "We're not hamsters. Why don't you come in?"

Lisa let them take an impression of her plastic, laminate her Polaroid in a membership card, assign a fitness trainer. She could only think how distracted David must have been in this salon of cosmetic hustle, listening for telltale signals from inner machinery.

"You lost someone," she said.

Her accusation floated away on the trainer's menu. "Weights, stairs, treadmills, sauna, steam. No one starts without a physical assessment."

After her orientation a cab was called to take her back to the shop, where voice mail from David's landlord asked for the names of immediate family, anyone who could clean out the apartment. "A Miss Despair was here. I didn't let her in."

Messages were coming from all over. There was a surprising new interest in her stock. David's death notice had moved quickly across the trade, an electronic whisper, carrying all the way to San Francisco. People she'd never heard from before were boldly solicitous. And Margot returned to wander in the stacks alone, unable to find what she was looking for.

Reaching the landlord, Lisa could only tell him what David had said. "The nearest relatives were books." It was lost on an ear deaf to sentimental riddles.

"He didn't even have his own transportation," the man said wistfully.

She understood what was meant: Why bother with formalities? Come and clean the place out yourself.

Sitting on his apartment floor, surrounded by dirty clothes, scattered corn chips, and an open container of bean dip that had grown a dark patina, Lisa found a single carton of books, which she removed to The Endless Shelf. There, with her doors locked, and bibliographies at hand, she unwrapped seventeen carefully preserved volumes.

She was all evening at it, checking her reference books, adrift in grand numbers. Every one a first edition, and most of them their author's first published works. The oldest, pristine in soft leather, Walton's *Compleat Angler*, London, 1673; the three-volume *Sense and Sensibility*, London, 1811, guaranteed a first by the four-fifths inch rule under the half title in volume one.

She thought of David caressing Lawrence's *Carchemish* and Kipling's *Schoolboy Lyrics.* By the time she got through to the Americans at the bottom, she nearly missed the last, protected in a flattened cereal box, the thin sheets of *Twilight*, Frost's first effort from Lawrence, Massachusetts, 1894, only two known copies.

Lisa could find no fault with the health club. They were careful taking her history, monitoring pulse and pressure of her first trip on the stationary bicycle, prescribing a measured regimen. And the members were encouraging—the solid and soft—generous to each body among them as a worthy project. Even the ones who swaggered back and forth between the weights and water cooler with patent lies like, "You're getting there," as she panted in place on her treadmill.

Her investigation turned up nothing. At the end of her first month her numbers were improving on the scales and charts. She'd always believed a body should bulk and decay on its own dignified schedule. Now, what had begun as a challenge to the health club was becoming a pleasurable duty. And reward followed exertion— the sauna, where she let the tears of her sad season run from every pore, and finally, the spa, shared with rosy faces ranged in a bodiless circle over the water.

Lisa assumed Margot continued at the health club for a meaner purpose. To flaunt her figure, to challenge and compare, still clinging to a claim on David's affection. Just as in the shop where her scavenging continued for "things that meant something to David."

Sitting across from her in the spa one evening, Lisa wondered what catchy fungus might be seeping into the water from Margot's direction. The air, too, polluted with her overheated recollection.

"David loved it in here. Yes, when we were alone he liked to slip his trunks down and let the jets of water play on his privates."

With that, Margot rose and came hand over hand through the bubbling pool until she was talking down into Lisa's face.

"You're surprised? What I want to know is why the landlord let you into his apartment."

Returning to her place across the spa, she sat again with her eyes rolled back, seeming content for the moment to have water as her fondling partner. "You never paid him a living wage," she accused. "How did you think he managed?" As if she knew the answer, and Lisa ought to be able to guess it. Absorbed in herself again, Margot was looking down, admiring her breasts floating smartly on the bubbly current.

Lisa would no longer answer presumptuous mail—or respond to the implication that she was privy to the D'Espere library. There was more rudeness from Mr. Stevey in Charleston. He was baiting her.

Are you responsible for rekindling the rumor of a "Ricus Adams"? Did you know that sightings of this ghost book have been a long-standing joke in the trade, a joke started by the deceased Mr. Seaton? I can tell you that Harvard has no record of a classmate of Adams called Ricus. And that they have never had a letter of intent from anyone to will such a volume to them. When you do a catalogue of the D'Espere collection, please send us a copy.

Most of the trade seemed to know Lisa had been chosen to receive the D'Espere library, and they couldn't understand why. The eventual summons to view the collection came from the widow like an invitation from another decade.

"High tea's at five. You'll have to be out of here by then."

Her directions led to a wood in far suburbia and a stone dwelling of late grandiosity. Mrs. D'Espere, quick in her eighties, was in full control of her household. When Lisa entered, Margot appeared in a bathrobe at the top of the stairway, but retreated at the first sound of her mother's voice.

"I told you to stay out of this."

Lisa was led through a dark hallway into a far grander room than she'd expected. Beautifully proportioned with a fireplace at one end, dark mahogany casing, and golden light filtering through parchment shades. There were two Morris chairs and a globe on tilted axis in a rosewood stand—the world as it turned in 1922—all laid on the wine and blue of a generous Persian rug.

"Two of my children were more interested in the nursery books," Mrs. D'Espere explained. "A tear or two for the childhood stories. *Babar, Junket Is Nice*, that sort of thing. Let's be honest, I've had others in before you. I was told you're not so particular, that you'd be willing to take the lot."

It was a gentleman's collection, gathered perhaps in the first half of the century, but spotted everywhere with latter-day intrigue and license. Titles ending in *Brief, Affair, File*. Bodice rippers and pleasure manuals all thrown in with the rest, and arranged by color and size, as if by the dust maid.

The Francis Parkman histories sat next to a matching blue how-to of sexual fulfillment, a pair of Twains embraced *Love's Picture Book*, and several Trollopes made ménage with illustrated G spot advice. It was as if the better society of the room had been carelessly exposed to social diseases, all of them picked up by Margot at The Endless Shelf.

Lisa saw herself collecting the whole pile again, a pile littered with her own base discards. Now she went about the room touching suede and vellum. Thackeray, Austen, Zola, Lamb, Dryden, Hugo, Stevenson, all in leather. Perhaps eight feet in all. At three hundred dollars per foot from Lucas Leather she'd be clear at twenty-four hundred.

Lisa moved quickly. A tired lot of stuff, she could say quite honestly. For Mrs. D'Espere she remarked on reprints from the nineteenth century, interesting authors in inferior editions with yellowing pages, and first editions of trash, things nobody collected anymore. A decimated set of the Harvard Classics leaned against one another, soldiers of a lost cultural war, with unconvincing presumption on their spines: "a library in a five-foot shelf."

"Twenty-five hundred," Lisa said. "Out of your way in a week."

"Because it all has to go," Mrs. D'Espere told her, leading her back through the hall. On the way out, the widow took her arm boldly and whispered, "I know what the three of you were up to. Well now you can clean up the mess you've made."

But the missing books, whatever they were, and their odious replacements were only a secondary irritation to her. She was rich beyond the scale of small thousands her husband's collection might have brought her. Her first concern was her daughter's predicament. And now she was speaking loud enough to be heard on the upstairs landing.

"A souvenir child is bound for an unhappy life, don't you agree, Miss Raimond? Has Margot told you I've arranged a long vacation for her?"

Lisa was shown out the front door, and Mrs. D'Espere was signaling end of conversation and good-bye, waving just the fingers of one hand.

By then it was obvious to Lisa she'd been called there to be humiliated. First to witness the depravity of the ravaged library, then to entertain the widow as Lisa played the crafty tradesman. And, in so many words, she'd been told that one germ too many had been spread from her Endless Shelf. That Margot was pregnant!

She had always been fair to her clients. But why should she justify herself to the contemptible widow who had nothing but contempt for her in return? Lisa was living now on forty thousand dollars from the sale of the Frost juvenilia. Little enough compensation, she thought, for everything she'd endured.

Again, why should she justify herself? It would be more to the point to say that her two rare birds had only been using her for cover, that a few rare volumes were her due for their betrayal—the lucky remains in the nest they'd fouled. And now Margot had been sent off by her mother to Arizona, even before she began to show.

Lisa waited till the following fall to tell her father she didn't want or need the usual year-end supplement. With just a hint to Caulkins, bidding on her perfect Izaak Walton had spiraled up to a marvelous figure.

She was doing very well. She'd hired another man, and they wouldn't tolerate a nuisance in the store. Reputations in the business were so easily driven by whispers. The others still wanted to know if Lisa held the Ricus Adams. They'd tried every trick to pry it loose. Even denied its existence. But the lovely thing was evidence enough of its own authenticity. It needn't be shown to anyone.

Lisa had been forced to imagine a child conceived under the dirty spell of her own shelves' love manuals, Margot off to a hospital to bear it, and even allowed to take it home. And the intervening months put a new color on David's ashes. All that elbow room in the overlarge grave, ample space for a transformation, a cracked urn and the chalky residue of her pure bookman became the common clay of a furtive procurer, a clandestine trader.

Stevey, from Charleston, was still trying to break her down.

Does it really matter whether David's bibliomania was a crime or a disease? I'd like to apologize for what my partner said to you, that you flinch whenever the word "provenance" is uttered.

Her store was secured by secrets now, by books nowhere to be seen. The best were spread around her house in chests and closets, under key. Caulkins was mad for the Walton, sweetening his offer with two Jefferson signatures, promising a start for her in Americana autographs. His figure was fine, but awkward in this tax year. She thought of Margot somewhere trying to add another name to a shrinking list of disgusted baby-sitters, hanging on in another bookshop. Probably climbing again on the collapsing stairs. Remaking herself into the taut sexual reed of premotherhood.

It was another year and a half before Lisa actually saw Margot. She'd been waiting all that time for her to make trouble about the books. But expectation was stood on its head. Margot had allowed flesh to thicken over her body in unselfconscious and pleasing measure. She was wearing a prim white blouse and loose jumper with a sash dropped below the waist, where it couldn't be tightened for vanity.

She appeared in the shop without warning and relaxed immediately into reminiscence, as if there had never been a quarrel between them.

Her child?

The doctors had explained it to Margot this way: If you believe something strongly enough, your body will pretend for a while that it's so. A phenomenon associated with grief. In fact she had never been pregnant.

"Not that we didn't give it a chance."

Still holding on to that much of David, she seemed honestly pleased to hear how well it was going for Lisa, here on the edge of profitable rumor, where no catalogue of her holdings was necessary. It was all internet now. Everything had changed.

"You were always so trusting," Margot said. "Letting us scavenge as we pleased."

Generous in her recasting of history in Lisa's favor, though the late discovery of charm couldn't really carry into the past. She and David were fixed in Lisa's memory in a sly hide-and-seek of book and flesh, while she came on behind them, prospering, unaccountable.

No need to chat with the other dealers. Next time a need arose, the modem could stay warm, dealing off another prize. The Adams, read and absorbed along with the stinging rebukes of its first reader, was in her bureau, a treasured sachet of distinctive mustiness, suffusing her underthings with a scent of age and honor.

It was not for sale. She liked holding the weight of its honest quarrel in her hands. Hanging on to the book, no matter what price was offered, gave an innocence to her saleable hoard. She felt free to reinvent herself, as if the subtlest possibilities of the trade, and her reputation in it, still beckoned from all directions.

Musical phrases, even conversation,
came to him in Mr. Morse's patterns.

5

Morse Operator

It's rat-a-tat-tat and then some, Russell tapping the kitchen table with a spoon. An attack of Morse. No message, just the alphabet, proving the dots and dashes are still available to him.

Across the room a televised map split the Soviet Union from a monolith of red into a dozen pastel pieces. All those years of American spying, and Russell's own tour in army intelligence, the source of his code, all for a flawed report of Russian economic brawn.

Russell had only transcribed a few messages long ago. Someone else had been busy all this time turning data on its head. Still, the code remains indelible, as if his synapses have been forever stamped *government property*. Now his finger tapping is the drumwork of reverie, and a reminder of the friend who came home with him across the ocean.

It's been thirty years since he drifted out of college and volunteered for army security. A ditty-picker, they'd called him. He'd wanted the language school in Monterey. Instead they force-fed him the Morse in Massachusetts, ignoring requests for transfer.

After several months of practice receiving signals through earphones and leading them to the keys of a typewriter, Russell had felt something like a machine. At first he had to think *di dah, A, left hand, little finger.* Then the sounds had begun to transfer themselves to paper without the advice or consent of his nervous brain. When the noise stopped at the end of a transmission, it took his fingers a few moments to catch up with his ears' memory.

What was the big secret if they were teaching him an international code? Shut up and listen, he was told. You don't have the need to know yet. They were making him a very fast operator, by far the fastest in his class.

During his total immersion Russell noticed that musical phrases, even conversation, came to him in Mr. Morse's patterns. Not just the most familiar, like · · ·—, V, for the opening of Beethoven's Fifth, but —·— —, Y, for a simple "How do you do." A few years later, when voices sang, "Good day, sunshine," he received —·—·, C, while others heard the Beatles.

Other responses, too, became reflexive, such as "Can't say," when people asked what the army was doing with him. And "It's classified," when his family pried. He could only tell them "England." He was warned of agents in the field who'd play on his vanity. "The cold war can burn you. It's dry ice." This, too, had fallen into singsong, "Don't betray yourself," dah di dah di dah.

They sent him to Yorkshire in September 1961. He found the moors lovely, not bleak as in literature. Their subtle shading and gentle inclines led the eye toward misty horizons. Their distances, so difficult to judge, made space a riddle that could only be solved by long walks. But something forbade walking on the moors, perhaps their lack of cover.

After work he and his mates used the pubs, soaking loneliness in ale. In the evenings a bus took the off-duty men from their signal base to the bottom of the nearby town, and they did their crawl, starting under a Watneys Red Barrel and working their way up the hill for a Bass in the big hotel.

Young women, the town's demimondaines, awaited their arrival, shift by shift, sipping limed gin in the bars. And still younger girls shimmied against the jukeboxes in below-the-street coffee clubs. Russell supposed the friend he might fancy was across town, behind the gates of the tennis club, where soldiers from the American camp were not welcome.

Right off, one of the publicans spotted him for a new man.

"Occupation forces, eh?" The man stood him a pint, and tried him.

"I suppose you boys do your share in that building with no windows."

Turning away from the bartender, he saw a familiar face. The man said his name was Paul, and wanted to know if Russell had met any women here, then talked on and on about himself. Liked his work, even wore his earphones into the mess hall, but admitted to problems in the service. The sleeves of his fatigues showed darker shades of olive drab, where various insignia of enlisted rank had been sewn on and then stripped away. Now he wore the single stripe of a private, same rank as Russell.

"I hear you're fast," Paul said when their eyes met in the mail line.

"Nothing to write home about."

"Better not." Paul winked. "No, I've heard about you."

Russell had been waiting for the moment to tell someone, "Reflexive speed is mindless speed."

"Never mind that. They'll find out how good you are and make you prove it."

For a while they were put to work in the same room at adjacent desks. But soon Paul was gone to another shift, and his prediction came true. The section chief was arranging a contest between Russell and the swiftest old hand around. They'd play tape-recorded code for the two of them, increasing the speed until one faltered. He couldn't back out; too many people counting on him.

Russell's actual mission was intercepting and tran-
scribing signals available to anyone with a radio—the
commercial traffic between European capitals sent by
high-speed Morse. Call letters and frequencies of the sta-
tions he monitored were listed in a thick volume published in Bern, Switzerland, for all the world to read.

Russell knew that other things were happening here
as well—interceptions of coded signals arising from
military maneuvering in Eastern Europe and from the
telemetry of Russian space shots. But he knew none of
the details. He sat in a friendly country recording the
business chat of other men and nations.

From one day to the next he might learn how many
watch movements were being shipped from Geneva to
Stockholm, or which functionary from Zagreb was arriving that night in Budapest. In slack periods he and
his friends played a game. One of them recited call letters, and someone else had to name the cities the letters were assigned to.

Russell bought a little English sedan, priced and en-
gineered for export, steering column on the left. And
shortly afterward, Paul got an almost identical model.

"How do you like mine?"

Not quite the same blue. Was he trying to be a twin,
or just envious of Russell's widening travels, which by
then included the Lake District, Scarborough, and several abbeys?

On an overnight trip to the lakes he saw the twin
car parked next to his bed-and-breakfast cottage. And

there was Paul winking across the dining room. Russell worried how he'd parry an intimate gesture without offending. Paul sat at his own table and left the inn without speaking.

A friend of Paul's was being sent home—it wasn't clear why. A security problem of some kind. The evening before the code contest Russell sat in the enlisted men's bar, where the two of them were having a last drink together. He heard Paul consoling the man.

At the contest the room was full. A crowd pressed around Russell's desk. He sat to his typewriter and proved himself something of a miracle operator. Code came, and his fingers moved unbidden over the keys. He kept his mind out of it. The opponent fell away at thirty-six words a minute, with Russell gaining speed as the tape broke. Still no telling how fast he might be.

Paul came out of the crowd to place a soft hand on his shoulder.

"Amazing," he said. "I'll make a fortune on you."

Way out of place in that room, where fellow soldiers were shouting promises of liquid reward in the evening ahead for their new champion. Morose in his victory, it was all the clearer the sort of equipment he'd become, a kind of metabolizing teleprinter surrounded by a cadre who took their work so seriously, Russell was isolated from any sympathetic intelligence. He was the restless agent of his country's vain secrecy, and his urge to tap Morse on a Harrogate bar was almost Tourettic.

It was no secret from himself that what he sought in his wandering over the moorlands and through the pubs of the Lake district was the lady friend who would repaint the north of England from a darker, romantic palette. All he'd managed thus far was a tiresome soldier dogging his heels. In the weeks that followed, Paul seemed to make a game of stalking Russell's off-duty wandering. His shadow everywhere. Russell wanted to leave all this, to go questing for new friends somewhere no one knew him.

In the spring he began to travel out through the hills once more, north and west. Paul couldn't be shaken. On another trip to the lakes, the man had appeared out of the bushes by Wordsworth's cottage, as if surprised to see a comrade in that alien countryside, clapping him on the back, with a cheery, "Nothing here but poets' ghosts."

One smooth line, and off again.

For a furlough Russell chose Norway in February. And first day out he fell in love. Three times. Once with a woman climbing past him as he descended the gangplank of the boat that brought him from Newcastle to Bergen, once with a willowy figure who stood on the railroad platform with a child—both of them waving to someone else—as his train pulled out of Bergen for Geilo, then in the bar of his little ski hotel.

Her name was Anske. For après-ski she wore a jumpsuit of umber velour. Curling and uncurling her toes in fleece-lined reindeer moccasins, she was in rapid conversation with her friends, almost breathless in her Scandinavian language; he could not say which. She spun on her bar stool and in unencumbered English asked Russell, "Don't you think so?"

"You were listening," she went on. "I didn't know if you could understand. I was saying it used to be the heart that was last to go. It worked harder when there was other disease in the body. Now it usually gives up first."

Anske was the dark one in her party, hair shiny black and skin close to olive. Very much the off-color berry in a harvest of blond. Her slate eyes danced with the mischief of a sudden friendship, while the others shrank from her presumption.

"Oh, Anske!" The women covered their mouths.

Later, in his room, before they got to last names, home cities, she wanted to know if Russell had traveled before in Europe, and what did he think of the struggle between the world's competing economic systems?

She went on in the same fetching, if philosophical, manner, stretched out on his comforter, and blinking, not at him, at the ceiling. She was rolling her shoulders and neck in the shiny nest of her raven hair, making a comfortable place for her busy mind.

"Americans," she said. "I think you take life, you take existence not quite seriously. Yet you are sentimental. You didn't come here for winter sport."

Then she was laughing at herself. "My friends call me the *cérébrale*. You know, a woman who needs only the company of her own brain. It isn't true."

She said it was hard to believe he'd come all that way to ski in the darkest month. Could she see his passport?

"Right now?"

"You'd like me to leave."

"No," he said, "you were explaining."

She sat up. "We were in the bar, my friends and I. Talking in our own language. You looked so lonely. And now you are amazed I am here on your bed."

"No," he lied. He *was* amazed by her perfect English.

"I've been to England," she said, falling back again, her arms stretched overhead, reaching for complete relaxation, inviting him down beside her.

He woke later to the sound of his door closing, and rolled over to gather all that was left of her body's warm print in the bed. In the morning he had salty fish and a croissant. At the front desk the manageress gave him a sheet with village activities of the week numbered one to three, and a little map showing where to rent skis and the location of the ski school.

"Anske, who was here last night with the others," he said. "Has she gone out yet?"

The woman said something to her husband in the office behind her, and they laughed together.

Russell had felt an honorable triumph over his long celibacy, as if Anske had offered herself as a welcome-to-the-country gift. And no gracious way to refuse it. How wise he'd been to come here, to a place where there was so little hypocrisy, where even the hotelkeepers smiled on a sudden romance under their roof. They must have been secretly happy for him. Secure at last in his anonymity, he could look ahead to two weeks of Norwegian vitality and warmth.

Outside for the first time in daylight he saw the steep mountains that cradled the village. A sign warned of avalanches. At the ski school he claimed parallel turns, called himself an intermediate, then crossed his skis trying to prove it and was put with beginners.

That afternoon he made great progress, with compliments from a boisterous woman who kept falling at his feet. "Edge with the skis," the instructor insisted, "edge with the skis," —· ·—, X. It was snowing, but across the dim landscape he could see small children lined up for turns on a great ski jump—tiny brave souls.

At dark he coasted down to his hotel where the manageress and her husband were fussing over their scarce company. When they asked how he liked the cheese they were serving, it only reminded him that he'd sliced from the same hard brick at the noon smorgasbord.

After dinner he was called into the office. The manageress let her husband begin. "There is a kind of lady coming here," he said, "not the best kind."

"No," the manageress said. "He will not understand. Not the for sale kind."

She described for Russell a set of women thought by the Geilo innkeepers to be bad for the village. Girls from Oslo, sometimes further. "In a place for nice families," she said, "they make trouble. And come with their male friends, but they look for other fortune."

"Opportunity," her husband thought a better word. "So you have a nice time here. She is no longer with us."

He gave Russell a postcard the young woman had left for him.

"We missed you this morning," it said. "Your friend, Anske."

The picture on the other side was of another hotel. Russell bought a thick sweater on display in the lobby, and with woolen snowflakes and reindeer prancing around his chest, he left through a side door.

He found her easily. All the blond cohorts with her, three young women and four men. "We waited so long," she said. "My friends want to meet you," and taking Russell's hand, she led the group to a basement café for beer and dancing.

How were they all related? Were these bad women, after all, or just good women slandered?

"So provincial here," Anske said. "To get reservations we tell them we are coming with family. Do you like it here?"

Her question startled him. It was as if the previous night had been erased, and the two of them as a pair were a fresh and exciting possibility.

She began to explain herself. Her last name, Hasselsteiner, was German, though she was Swedish, and German was only one of her four languages. She wanted to know all about Russell. In English would be fine. She'd had a friend who had gone to Wyoming and come home with a husband from California.

"Do you play the drums?"

He was beating a fingernail tattoo on the table, keeping rhythm with a concertina, —·—· — —·—, CQ, the network call.

Anske nodded her head to the beat. With the blessings of all, even the men, Russell had been welcomed into the party. Anske, no longer the *cérébrale*, was completely attentive, and he wondered at the ease of it, the lack of resistance from any quarter.

They all left together for the bar of another hotel. They were drinking pilsner, toasting countries, states, the French downhill champion of the season. There was waltzing.

"I'm an operator in the international radio," Anske told him. "In Stockholm."

"God!" he said. "You're YOJ 23!"

"But how could you know that?"

Flustered, he spent several minutes trying to explain it away as the chance knowledge of a radio ham. He couldn't make her understand, couldn't translate *ham*.

One of Anske's friends thought Russell might have called her a pig. She asked again to see his passport. The group's English had vanished, turned into guttural secrets.

Anske said something to one of them, who turned to him and demanded, "Who are you?"

The music stopped. At other tables, too, they were watching. Anske's friends were pulling her away from him, out of the room. Russell left for his own hotel.

In the morning he carried his skis onto the first gondola up the mountain. Partway up, the car halted and swung in the wind. Over nothing, as far as he could tell. And then he was at the peak, alone, the gondola starting its descent.

Skis clipped on, he looked down in terror at the fall line. With a false move it appeared he might hurtle all the way down to impale himself on a spire of the village.

He could sideslip for a way in one direction, but what use if he dared not turn himself directly down the mountain to traverse away from precipice or boulder? They would allow a man to move from here? The authorities, the insurance companies?

He edged forward, began to slip, and then he was tumbling. He'd fallen perhaps fifty yards before a loose ski became the anchor that dragged and finally stopped him.

It was a long time before he had his skis under him again and made fast to his boots.

As he stood he began to slip again. With the same result. Over and over. One knee was terribly sore; he'd twisted an arm. This was the only way down: sliding on his backside, then pinwheeling out of control until something caught and held.

He was standing, leaning on his poles, when Anske and her friends fell from the clouds. There was a piercing harmonic, "yo dul o dul o," turned *dah di dah di dah* by his army ear, and one of them dropped out of sight. Anske stopped a little distance below and called back.

"Are you fine?"

He raised a pole to reassure her.

"Wonderful, isn't it," she said, "the rhythm of descent?"

Exuberant in the crystalline world around her. Then she was off to catch the others, in free fall for a moment before the slope caught her once more. Left and right and left, her body swinging to the demands of gravity and the shape of the mountain, to a rhythm for which there was no analogue in his code.

The angle eased, the hill softened to a friendly powder. He began to admire the courage that had brought him down to an inhabited elevation, where other skiers darted around him, laughing, calling attention to their mastery of the piste.

He was going down to show Anske the little slip of paper, signed by a sergeant, that served as his passport. He might even confess his batty soldiering, the small beer of his daily intercept. If he explained himself fully, she could be warned to keep his silly little secret. He stood for a long while looking back at the summit, marveling again at his foolhardy accomplishment.

Skis on his shoulder, he limped down to his hotel where the manageress made over his injuries. She seemed pleased to be handing him a note from the young woman.

We are leaving for another village.

I will contact. Do you believe me?

He sank into a chair. Anske would have no idea where to find him. And the manager was whispering to him. "Trouble? A man here today with so many questions about you."

Russell was cutting his vacation short, leaving Geilo the next morning. On the trip back to Bergen he looked for an empty coach, but passengers were scattered all through the train. Once, coming down through the mountains, he made a fist to keep his fingers from turning the wheels' clickety-clack, · · ·—, into *V*'s.

From Bergen back to Newcastle he walked his ship's rail, wondering what the friend he had made in the mountains might be saying about him. At customs he was ready to declare nothing but his innocence. Looking down from the boat to the dockside parking lot, he saw the twin car parked next to his own. And sidling next to him at the rail, here he was again, the long arm of a too-easy friendship closing around his shoulder. And so coy.

"I met your friends. They said they didn't understand you. What was it you told them—you were in pig radio?"

They went to their separate cars, and Paul played bumper tag, with a foolish grin for Russell's mirror, all the way down to Yorkshire.

Back in camp, accusation hung over him. He saw himself before a board of officers who would cheapen and misconstrue. "A blond Swede? He jeopardized the mission for that?"

Would he answer, "Not blond, I told her nothing"?

They'd have no use for the awkward truth, that his outburst in Geilo—the Stockholm call letters—had been a kind of boast, a vain display, and really no more than a hint of his work here. And they'd have an ugly word for Anske.

With passing days, Russell fell back into an innocence confirmed by official silence. No one had accused him of spilling secrets. He whistled a lively sequence of dots and dashes—the network call—as he filled out forms for a leave to Stockholm, and a surprise reunion with Anske.

Another week. And the black call had come. Not quite as he'd imagined. The captain wished to see him.

Hurried by the company clerk, Russell arrived in the duty office out of breath, panicky. He was told to sit, to be at ease. A paper was thrust in his hands.

"Read this."

His eye caught something underlined in the middle of the typed sheet.

. . . no evidence confirming subject is homosexual
. . .

"No," the captain ordered. "From the beginning. All of it. Aloud."

"Subject promoted Specialist Fourth Class December, nineteen sixty-one. Receives proficiency pay. Under surveillance since arrival this station."

His voice was cracking, he swallowed.

"A loner. Negative attitude to mission? Travels off post. Mostly in country. Pubs, inns. Has engaged barmen in conversations critical of American politics, education, television."

"Can't you read without swallowing?"

"At Alexander Hotel, Harrogate, called U.S. President, 'a cortisone freak.' In Skipton pub agreed with British national, America too late entering WW Two. At Traveler's Rest, York Road, Joined Englishmen singing,

> *Our headmaster, he was such a fool,*
> *He only had a teeny-weeny tool.*
> *It was good for keyholes,*
> *And little girlies' pee holes, et cetera.*

Clues to sexual orientation? Came out door yelling 'God save the Brits.'"

At this point he began to read firmly, steadied by revulsion and anger.

"No evidence confirming subject is homosexual as alleged by Specialist Fourth Class XXXXXXX of same barracks, who was heard calling 'Hey, you homo.' Subject left without denying charge."

There was more about a book of poetry behind the inspection display at the top of Russell's closet. Then some lines about the Norway trip, and "a rendezvous with Swedish national who spent several hours in subject's room. Two days later pretended not to know one another."

"Well?"

"A gossip column," Russell called it.

The captain agreed. "Worthless. Soft as a sneaker full of shit. But I can't approve a leave to Stockholm. Not with this in your file. You can thank the man who wrote it. How does the rest of that song go?"

Two new soldiers wanted to challenge Russell for the code championship. He refused. At work he was slowing down on purpose, purging reflexive behavior, starting with the signals themselves. This meant thinking about the Morse characters as they went by, moving his lips to pronounce the words they spelled, like an old man reading.

Paul could occasionally be seen walking the perimeter of the camp, always alone. He was moved from the enlisted men's barracks into bachelor officers quarters, and even there, he seemed to be without company. No longer the friendly confidant.

"You couldn't be trusted," he told Russell one morning.

"What did I know? How could you waste all that time on me?"

"You were the pessimistic type," he said, "no sympathy for the mission. Whenever you made new friends, they had to be checked out, too."

The next week, Paul was gone, assigned somewhere in Germany. Easy then to forget all the insinuations as Russell nursed the promise made in Norway. When Scandinavian features began to drift, he had only to switch antennae. On the midnight shift, alert beside his receiver, he was gentle with the dial. And Anske came skipping through the air with perfect clarity, full of little secrets.

One night she revealed seven Volvos were on their way from Göteborg to London. On another, four bankers from her city were seeking audience with the Queen of Denmark. With patience, the small news of businessmen gave way to the business of romance. He was by his radio listening when the faithful pulse from Stockholm split the dark air into the letters of his name.

All but the Daisy Mao were ripe
as the pier they were tied to.

6

Leaving Port McHair

Karen, dressed to blend with woods and moss, was leaving to float the Mississippi from Memphis to the delta. Her boyfriend, Paul, with a new mustache dyed black and hair shorn to the scalp, was on his way to Canada with no suitcase or satchel, only a city for a destination. In the car he was reading aloud from a column in the *City Fist*.

"Mount bronze generals on horseback, and set them rearing in the traffic circles. Put out more flags. Trick her out as you will, from her political heart to muddy Potomac banks, she remains a city of deception and stagecraft.

"City? This is no city." Paul threw the paper down. "It's a pose."

"Nice," I said. "Do you have any money?"

"No."

I turned up Louisiana, sighting on the station's central arch, thinking even the avenues, set at obliques, aid deception in Washington. You can sneak up on the bronze generals, or in this case, Union Station, at an angle.

"There," Paul said, "take one of those."

"They're for congressmen."

Fleeing the country, he closed his eyes, disgusted. I parked in the illegal space, and walked with him into the station with a hand on my wallet, ready to pay for his escape, but couldn't help saying, "If you have no money for travel, you have no need to travel."

I was quoting Will, who'd been quoting Marx for us all month.

We settled onto one of those long, puritan station benches that allow upright sitting while opposing sleep, spilling recumbents on the floor. Paul began to work the huge room from where he sat, looking for a soft heart.

I was only five years older than Paul, but the gap could have been a generation. East and west, moods changed that quickly. I'd graduated in 1959 before a first long inhale had been drawn and held in Berkeley, before the first Freedom bus left a New England campus for Dixie. By the time Paul arrived in Cambridge for his freshman year a daily inhalation of secondary head smoke was a campus certainty. The North to South

Freedom line was as busy as Ho's jungle trail. And my sorry generation, five years out of college, had its retrospective label. Apathetic.

Early inoculation with hippy antibodies kept my fascination with Paul from crossing into imitation. That and my exposure to the idea of a less-than-inspired second coming, the rough beast slouching. I took my chance with enlistment only a few years before this became a life-threatening gamble.

Returning from my three-year tour at an army signal base in Yorkshire, I found America transformed; the young balking at every turn, refusing work, refusing the draft, refusing common fashion until this became fashionable itself. I stood back and watched, as bemused by the got-something-for-the-head stoners as I was disgusted by the socks-up posers with flags on their lapels. My sympathies were all with Paul's unbuckled freedom, but my instincts left me doggo on the sidelines.

It was curious how the next troubled years turned our heads in opposite directions. Mine toward the romance, if not the practice, of Paul's Movement, or his life at Port McHair, while his experiment with a purposeful poverty and protest had transformed him into a crafty and shameless survivor, and now, a fugitive. I teased his excess; he exposed my lack of passion.

As we sat side by side in the terminal, what I saw was the vaulted ceiling of a grand station at one end of the continent. And a broad slanting panel of mote-laden air carrying sunlight from sixty feet overhead all the way to the floor, blessing Paul's departure. But Paul saw the same great concourse illuminated by a solar interrogation lamp that found and fixed him in its wide track, and a palatial tollhouse placed between him and the steel rails radiating across the country, with police patrolling every gate and doorway.

With Paul in flight to Montreal and Karen on her way to the Mississippi, I remained tied to duty in an actuarial office, though the risks that really interested me were the kind these two were taking with their lives. They'd been living together on a small, derelict cabin cruiser that Paul converted into a floating apartment.

Moored at the Buzzard's Point marina at the bottom of the city, where a finger of the Anacostia River meets its main channel and joins the Potomac, the boat rose and fell with the Chesapeake's tide. It was one of nine disabled craft that were home to this disaffected community known along the waterfront as Port McHair, after the neighboring army barracks of Fort McNair.

There were seven soft-hulled cabin cruisers in the fleet, plus a salvaged PT boat, two sailboats with neither boom nor mast, and a newcomer—a rigged, cabined sailer, the *Daisy Mao*. The freeboards of most were mottled with peeling paint and algae. They were ripe as the pier they were tied to, and none seemed capable of self-propulsion, though Paul and his friends spoke frequently of seaworthy futures and faraway ports.

There had been a relaxed communal season at Port McHair when the residents could visit one another at any time of day. Any lonely cabin had been part of a nine-room houseboat whose separate decks were stepping-stones to neighbors and a shortcut to the central dock. As time passed privacy and order reasserted themselves.

Now there was Daisy on her *Daisy Mao*. She tied up in a slip in the middle of the line, and spoke to no one for several days. All along the dock the curious residents waited for a sign of Daisy's colors. These were eventually shown to be friendly and without modesty; not a flag, but a laundry of blouse, jeans, and underthings pinned out to dry on her lifelines.

When she finally emerged from her cabin, Paul said her first question was, "Where does the sewage go?" Into the churning ebb and swell of the river, but this was the last thing you'd ask at McHair if you knew anything about the place. Eviction for environmental impact was a constant threat. The docks were on federal property leased to an absentee whose rents were collected by an amiable superintendent, Roy, who assisted her as he would any newcomer, with a pump and wrench, and the whispered advice, "Pump your tanks at night."

Roy lived on the *Queen Mary*, a garbage scow retired from the Manhattan-to-Staten Island run. Its spongy hulk listed to shore, and the hum of a bilge pump under its square cabin was the white noise that helped the community to sleep against an occasional horn on Water Street.

It was stylish in the counterculture as Paul and the others practiced it to take advantage of everything bourgeois, everything and everybody, and to call this liberation—a simultaneous cleansing of property and the national spirit. It was part of the revolution that so many talked about, with sorry consequence for karmic sin, not just political obtuseness or rapacious greed, or pocking the Vietnam delta from high altitude, but any shade of mind complacent with the "quo."

It was not only acceptable on an August evening in 1967 that Paul should be stealing lobsters from the refrigerated shed behind the Water Palace Restaurant, but something like a moral obligation. Karen, who said yes to this man, was in the ferment of a rebellion within the Rebellion. She was on their punky craft, the *Sea Something*, where she and the lobster thief kept house in the boat's refitted cabin, lighting the charcoal for the evening's plunder.

Paul had rigged the dock-bound vessel with a hot water heater. Under a trapdoor in the floor was a clawfoot tub you could soak in, with your head in the cabin and legs under the planking. A fold-down table, a hotplate and a motley of cups, plates, and utensils wedged on one wall turned the dayroom-study-curtained head into a galley. Two bunks were forward in V-formation at the bow.

All this for forty-five dollars a month—slip, water tap, and hundred-and-ten socket. Life on the water with ginger-haired Karen seemed enviable, and admirably simple. Leggy and self-assured at twenty-four, Karen was fierce in her love, or so Paul said. With his own soft round face under brown curls, he was solid with her that season against any who remarked on her cosmetic attraction before her inner worth.

"I didn't fall in love with the man," she said, "I fell in love with his revolutionary spirit."

Karen's heart was already ashore and traveling, and the rest of her would be leaving soon. At the equinox—because she still meant to prove to him she could stand an egg on its end at the moment when the seasons were perfectly divided—a demonstration of the cosmic balancing act that held everything in place. More likely it was her lighthearted way of easing the shock of abandonment. Looking back, it's easier to see them both struggling for political respect in an era of angry opposites, and unaware as one of Karen's eggs how unequal was the balance between the emotional power of their movement and the actual power of the state.

Not two but three lobsters that night, because there was apt to be company—me, tooling down from my bourgie nine-to-five in midtown. Paul had been late getting to the seafood shack, delayed at a meeting where some would-be writers and editors met to plan a new journal. When I arrived at the marina, I found a stranger already onboard the *Sea Something*. He was telling Karen how impressive her man had been at the meeting, the only one who seemed to appreciate the real depth of Marx's thought.

"Paul's never read Marx," she told him.

The young man was very excited, sure that he and Paul had more to talk about, not just the obvious dialectic, but Marx's theories on all human relations, not the least of these, love.

"Marx?" she said. "Love?"

"Of course."

Karen flinched as she turned and saw me, as if I might embarrass her in front of her new friend.

"What are you doing here? This is Will," she said. "He's with Daisy on the *Daisy Mao*. I've asked him for supper."

The coincidence of Will showing up at Paul's meeting and then in the middle of Port McHair was, in Karen's mind, another demonstration of grace, and her conundrum. "There are no coincidences." She was making it clear I'd be one mouth too many that night, eating and talking.

More discouraging, the once elusive Daisy, whom I thought might be a free heart in the community, already had a live-aboard other in her life, this reedy Marx enthusiast with a gold-capped front tooth. Her *Daisy Mao*, freshly painted with a stenciled ring of red daisies around the hull, had seemed an unlikely addition to the dock, but now it all fit.

And I didn't.

Perhaps Karen thought she was being kind, making clear I wasn't expected for dinner, maybe sparing me the whole Manifesto, thinking I might gag on the night's conversation, or say something awkward. As if she and Paul were red-dyed Socialists. Actually Karen nibbled at the edge of capitalism, going uptown twice a week to write business notes for the trade journal *Ice Cream Monthly*.

"Any scoops today?" was Paul's tease, and she welcomed it. To defend the job would acknowledge the grip, however faint, of the Establishment on her life. Paul made deliveries in a van acquired at a navy yard auction. He moved parcels for people who paid in cash, off the books. Establishment. Funny how the word got lost in the years that followed, disappeared, as a sure thing disdains its own redundant name.

I stayed only long enough that evening to greet Paul when he came aboard with the lobsters, and to hear Will praise him again for his performance at the meeting. Before stepping onto the dock I asked, "What was it about Marx and love?" If I was leaving, Will said, there wasn't time to explain, but it had to do with the confusion of love and self-infatuation; if I was really interested, he could show me several essays Marx and Engels had written together.

"I can tell you this," he said. "When the bourgeoisie are no longer content having the daughters of the proletariat at their disposal, they seduce each other's wives."

Paul was asking me to stay and share, but I knew Karen expected me to decline. As I made my way off the boat, Paul called to me. "So stick to the daughters of the proletariat!"

Neither of us was close to any daughter of the proletariat. Karen's parents made a nice living importing Italian shoes, Paul's father sold cleaning solvents for tanker trucks, and the short list of young women I'd be calling to join me that evening—in vain—all carried plastic.

There had been no way to call ahead. Port McHair's only telephone in those days was in the cabin of Roy's scow, served by a sagging line from a pole in the parking lot. And Roy would not be used as a messenger. My visits to the *Sea Something* were always a gamble. If Paul and Karen were ashore, I'd made the trip for nothing, and if Karen was there alone, the two of us had to strain a little for civility.

"No, stay," she said, the next time I came by.

A canned bugle was blowing retreat on loudspeakers over the parade ground at Fort McNair. Karen said Paul and Will were at another meeting. The journal idea had been abandoned, she told me. The same cell of propagandists had voted to let larger presses tell their story. And the story was more civil disobedience. A blockade of the avenues? Trash cans set afire and rolled into the streets? It seemed like small mischief daring a measured reprisal.

Kindness of television, everyone had seen the long manes of the rascals flying behind them as they fled from angry police in a war of middle fingers and billy clubs. Humdrum in retrospect, but if there was a pathetic miscalculation of possibilities, the thud of club to skull was real enough. Tactics were under discussion that evening, and Will's last Marxian lesson had impressed Karen, who was pleased to quote him for me.

"Too much philosophy is satisfied with its own cleverness. The proper goal of philosophy is to change the world."

She invited me to sit and wait for Paul. We dangled our legs over the side of the boat and let the lapping water fill the silences between us. If Karen had been moved by Will's teaching, she hadn't been persuaded to attend the meetings on the lawn of the one university in Washington where no one would have thought to look for them—in that void of political activity, far off by Ward Circle; no one perhaps but a lone security man, who would have taken them for the aimless academic cattle of summer grazing on any available campus.

Daisy waved to us from the deck of the *Daisy Mao*, where she was hanging her clothes to dry again, though Will had apologized to all of us for his lady's casual habit. Two slips away we could hear Raoul Kress's Underwood, another screed rolling up the platen for the *City Fist*. Little matter to him that the editors paid a pittance and so grudgingly. He had thirty thousand dol-

lars to work off, interest still accruing, before the tax-
men were finished with their garnishee on his earnings.

Kress, gray whiskered and rheumy at forty, was one
Port McHair resident with actual political experience,
and ideas he could spell. Veteran of a presidential campaign, his libertarian rhetoric rang with the Greco-
Kennedy echo, but shot from the hip in the campaign,
it proved fatal to his own candidate.

In forced political retirement Raoul floated in cama-
raderie with the rest of the marina. But his life seemed
dreary to me, without prospect of pleasure. His marriage clattered along, as noisy as his typewriter. His
wife, Cretia, nervous and stray haired, kept him on
edge with a thin collection of Sappho by her bunk. She
had a yappy little mutt that stuck to her side, aware of
the ill will it invited beyond its own decks. Cretia could
be found from time to time with the dog in anyone's
empty bunk along the row, a bit of sleeping trouble,
which it was best not to wake.

"That book you gave Paul. It's a piece of crap," Karen
said, and she told me why: the only woman in it, a
complaisant wife, offers herself, kneeling and without
enthusiasm, to a husband who's off in the morning on a
mannish whitewater trip."

"Fiction," I said. "You can't assume the author—"

"Bullshit," she said. "Are you staying for supper?"

I don't think she ever forgave me for once referring
to her as a girl. Perhaps she was right about that, too.
But *lady*? I just couldn't.

Paul and Will came back at dusk with several cases of beer, a big package of hamburger meat, and a bag of charcoal, none of it liberated, all cash purchases. These were Will's gifts to an impromptu party. Celebrating what? Paul went deck to deck, inviting every floating neighbor.

"Of course you're staying," he told me.

When the charcoal was ready, the big lump of hamburger meat was still sitting untouched beside the hibachi on the dock—Karen's passive resistance to the evening. She didn't need to say, "I'm not making them." Cretia said it for her, calling from the front bunks where she and Karen had their heads together, letting the men finish what they started.

"Karen's not making them!"

Roy came surefooted down the rickety dock from the *Queen Mary* with a blast on his foghorn-in-a-can. Two more heads lifted like periscopes from their hatches, swiveled to the *Sea Something*, and rose to the occasion; Bess Crane and Webber Gaunt, a love match made at McHair. They came across the other boats with the slow, three-point progress of mountain climbers.

"Pot legs will never be sea legs," Roy said, and he began to sing softly. "Just seventeen, in a dirty old dress, but a conscience so clean . . . "

"She's not dirty," Paul said. "She has gypsy skin."

Karen let Bess use the tub every Wednesday night when her week's patina gave way to a mottled rosy glow.

Bess worked in beach-glass jewelry. She had soldered herself with an innocent faith to Webber, who peddled dope in the new apartments in the southwest quadrant of the city.

I didn't notice when Billy Kasten arrived at the party. He had a way of sidling up out of nowhere, practiced in the Vietnam undergrowth and brought home to frighten us. From a graveyard of old liberty ships and sunken freighters closer to the bay, Kasten had raised and renovated the PT boat. Towed to McHair, it occupied the last slip in the marina, towering over the other craft, and jutting seventy feet into the river.

Kasten was disgusted with the war, with those who protested it, those who fought it, and those who made them fight. He wasn't ashamed to tell anyone he lived on a disability payment, but made a secret of the specific handicap. I came face to face with him in the cabin, where he was toasting two hamburger buns between the hot plate and Karen's iron.

All of us were guests on the *Sea Something* that evening, and before the night was over we were all restricted to the marina by the police. It wasn't till then we realized no one there knew Daisy's last name. Not even her friend Will, who claimed she carried no ID because she'd been running from something she dared not explain to anyone.

The party started with Will climbing onto the cabin roof and offering a toast to Paul.

"It'll take courage, but he's ready."

As if we were all privy to the plans they'd been making.

"What we have to remember is, 'events are only transitions, not significant in themselves,'" he said.

Billy Kasten spun around. A vein stood out like coaxial cable on his neck. "If your guts were spilled on the ground and had to be sewn back in your belly, would that be significant?"

"That would be an individual tragedy."

Billy leaped acrobatically from one intervening boat to the next, and climbed to his PT's deck, where he could comment on the proceeding without apology. He still had the necks of two beer bottles between the fingers of one hand, entitlements he didn't have to justify.

Will was going on with his peculiar homage to Paul.

"He's been carrying a load for all of us, brave as any fool in the Nam jungle."

"What about you?" Billy called down, as Will's toast soared toward nonsense, running away with him, into heroic mist.

"Don't worry about that. I'll be there."

What and where were still secrets between him and Paul.

"This idyll here," he went on, "this floating community of half-committed souls . . . I don't think Marx would approve. Remember, 'all figures of scenic presence are ideological shams of the ruling class. They frustrate the dialectical march to freedom.'"

Kasten called down to him. "Where do you work?"

"Here and there," he said. "I know what you're really asking is where my money comes from. About money, Marx teaches us this. It turns everything into its opposite. Love into hate. Virgins into whores. Loyalty into treason."

Kasten disappeared into his cabin.

"Come back. There's more," Will said. He was laughing at the retreat, and wetting his lips to go on, when Daisy ran a finger across her neck, and he climbed down from his podium. To mingle with us proles, I suppose. Later I caught him and Daisy smoking a cigarette in the forward bunks, as if they were offstage for a moment, and amused by something they wouldn't share with me.

Shamed by so much of Will's pessimistic wisdom, the company had begun retiring to their own boats after only an hour of partying. I sat with Paul long after the others left, listening to planes revving at the Naval Air Station across the water. Two lamps on the dock cast wavering lines into the river where they were met and driven back by runway lights on the distant airfield, giving silhouette to small craft moving down the Potomac.

Karen came out of the cabin and handed Paul a piece of paper.

"Did you write this?" she asked.

"It's for you," he said.

She put her arms around him from behind, snuggling against his neck. "Listen to this," and she read for me, "I could a thousand volumes fill, writing Karen in each line, Love is Karen, Karen is love's name."

"Marx wrote it," Paul confessed.

"For Jenny Von Westphalen. Before they were married," Will called over from the *Daisy Mao.*

We couldn't see him, didn't even know he'd been listening.

Karen was a little disappointed that Paul hadn't composed the lines himself. She went back to her bunk, and snuffed her sconce candle.

Paul and I were still sitting on the deck when he told me she was leaving in a few weeks. He was taking it bravely, transferring the emotion brimming in his eyes to his antiwar effort, explaining what an education it had been watching Will rein in the immature and diverse energy of floating university students, turning them in one direction. "He doesn't just talk the stuff, he puts it to work. You'll see, tomorrow."

"He smokes cigarettes," I argued. "Daisy too."

Paul insisted he was proud to be Will's deputy. He'd never met anyone who knew Marx in such detail, from the juvenilia to the serious stuff.

That's when we heard glass shatter, and the shouting started on the *Daisy Mao.*

The argument came up from the cabin into the open night. We saw Will climb to the deck in his shorts. She was right behind him in her underwear, flailing, pushing him backward.

"Bourgeois whore!" he called her.

"No little bastard is turning this into a marriage!" Daisy shouted back at him. "I told you, stay off me! Can't you understand that?"

Roy came down the dock with a flashlight and a tire iron. Bess hid her face in Webber's chest. Behind us, Cretia Kress called to Daisy. "Push him off!"

It was Daisy who went over the side. Not pushed, I think, but throwing her weight at him and continuing into the water when he stepped aside. Except for the ugly mood it was more like choreographed slapstick.

Instead of climbing back on her boat, Daisy was swimming away from the dock, right through the marina's bilge. She had her head right into it, doing the crawl.

"Go ahead! Make a scene! No one's watching!" Will called to her. Aside to Roy, he said, "Don't worry, she's a swimmer."

She turned and rolled onto her back, a Siren turned venomous, her voice carrying easily over the water, informing all of Port McHair, "Keep the boat, asshole. You couldn't sail a frisbee." And she was off again.

"She'll get tired," Will said. "She'll turn around. I think she's learned her lesson, don't you?"

She didn't turn. We could see her white hands windmilling into the Anacostia's mouth, and eventually into the receding tide of the Potomac. Then the hands, too, disappeared in the shadows of the fishing boats heading downriver to the bay for their morning run.

Roy didn't wait any longer to call for a police boat.

In the morning there were six craft searching, two of them dragging the bottom of the river.

Will kept saying he couldn't believe it, though he was the one who said he'd seen her go down for a third and last time, as if this were the only way a real drowning could happen, by the conventional numbers. None of the rest of us had seen it. Roy had to confess to the police that he'd taken his slip rental from her in cash, and allowed her to sign her lease as Daisy Daisy.

Shocked more than saddened, I kept uncharitable notions to myself: a cold, pretty, unpleasant woman taking a last turn in her bra and panties. An artificial, theatrical death. Eventually we could say without melodrama, "We never saw her again."

The police, knocking beer bottles out of their way, took statements that night from Will and Roy, then grew bored with the mournful, whispered testimony of others. They told the rest of us to be present for questions in the morning. Paul brought up a pillow and rigged a rope cradle to keep me from rolling into the river. I slept the few hours till dawn on his deck. The police never came back.

We assumed the protest planned for the afternoon would be canceled, but nothing of the sort.

"Events are only transitions," Will said once more, already burying tragedy under political zeal. We couldn't believe it, but he had things to do uptown in preparation for the afternoon. "We'll have a moment of silence for her this afternoon. That's the memorial she'd want. Are you coming this time?" he asked me.

I shook my head.

"I didn't think so," he said.

"He's got a job," Paul offered in my defense.

"That's the point," Will replied with his back to us, jumping off the boat, hurrying away with a light step for a grieving man.

"I'm coming with you," I told Paul.

He described a plan so simple, so tame, it made Will's fuss ludicrous. I had more anxiety about the workday I was missing. Three hundred volunteers were on their way to occupy the university's administration building, sneaking up on the bronze General Ward from the southeast, up Massachusetts Avenue on foot.

Paul was leader of the squad that would sit in the president's office. It was even easier in execution than theory; a dozen of us walked in, and the president walked out, with no time for our explanation. Staff throughout the building spilled from their offices without argument, with no more fuss than a receding tide at the pull of gravity, as the political imperative took its course.

Paul chained two of his men to the pipes in the president's bathroom. At a window I kept watch over the traffic circling the cloaked General Ward, the earlier revolutionary. No signs, no banners, no chant, just a deflating silence until we heard sirens coming toward us, up the same avenue. I watched a line of police cars and paddy wagons come flashing around the circle and onto the campus.

"What are you doing? Get away from there!"

It was Will in the office doorway, motioning me away from the window with a big black pistol.

"What's that?" Paul asked him.

He handed it by the barrel for inspection, and Paul's hand folded over the black grip as his finger slipped through the trigger guard.

"What do I need this for?"

"How else do you expect to hold the building?"

Paul was following him across the room, but Will was on his way out the door.

Paul was still staring at the unnecessary thing in his hand when two plainclothesmen entered the office, one with a drawn pistol of his own. Paul put the gun on the president's desk as ordered. They removed the clip and let the bullets clatter to the floor, looking around the room, confirming the attention of the rest of us.

They put the gun and bullets in a plastic bag. Paul was handcuffed and led away. We could leave the building or be arrested one by one. Of course we chose arrest, and were driven to the precinct station, fourteen to a wagon. Our fingerprints were taken and we were released.

There was no pleasure in telling Karen that Paul, as Will predicted, had been the day's martyr. Not for any action he'd taken, unless it was taking custody of the pistol. A week later, when she was finally allowed to visit him, he told her to follow Will's advice, he'd know what to do. But Will hadn't come back. Paul's bail was set at twenty-five thousand dollars, and who had that kind of bread?

At Port McHair, sympathy showered down on Karen. First, a forty-eight-hour sleepover and vigil by Cretia with readings from Sappho, interrupted by Bess, who made an emotional puddle everywhere she settled on the boat. Karen's eyes were never wet. She asked me to tell the commiseration squad "enough." And she sent me to tell Paul that Will was still avoiding the marina and the *Daisy Mao*.

Some of the men tried to be useful. Billy Kasten appointed himself Karen's handyman. Right away his attentions were upstaged by Webber, and soon everyone realized that Bess's misery was all about her own boat, because her Webber, assuming the gun felony charge against Paul had long-term consequences, was maneuvering to exchange his bunk for the one beside Karen on the *Sea Something*.

Raoul was busy at his Underwood, writing a piece on the role of women in the Movement, with a complimentary paragraph for Karen, though his actual story was set in a real city, where real blood was shed; his protagonist, a daughter of wealth and influence of whom nothing was left but a finger and its print, the aftershock of violence ineptly turned on itself.

Paul's father, as it happened, had that kind of bread, enough to credit Marx's axiom on money, enough to turn his son from an inmate into a free man—if only temporarily. Paul was back on the *Sea Something* with his trial set for November. He wasn't so much angry as he was ashamed of his trusting heart, and frightened by the prospect of a conviction. His freedom took me by surprise; he was phoning me from the *Queen Mary*.

"Come down here," he said. "I've got something for you."

Karen had moved up the date of her departure. Before the equinox, but not before she'd help him with his disguise. She asked if I'd give him cover on his flight from the District. I never hesitated. It was an impulse of solidarity, and not just with Paul, but with all of Port McHair.

I'll say this for Karen, she was honest with him. And with me. There was never any artful flirting. Faithful to a fault, until she decided to move on, and then she made a clean break, giving no quarter, and asking none. Her question to me was more like a challenge: Will you do this much, at least?

"No egg balancing?" I asked.

"That's bogus," Karen admitted. "You can do it any day of the year." She found a level place on the pier, and proved it to us, standing an egg on its end for a full minute. It was early September, two weeks before the equinox. We were sitting still as Yogis, marveling, when the egg tumbled over and rolled into the water. It might have stayed upright longer but for the two men jostling the dock as they stepped onto the *Daisy Mao*. Unlikely sailors, in dark suits and hard soles.

Friends of Will? We didn't know.

Rude beyond Billy Kasten's tolerance, he got their attention, proffering a whole arm for a middle finger. One of them looked up at Billy, then over at his mate, calm as Steiger playing Dillinger in an easy bank, and they went back to their business, firing up the *Daisy*'s engine and casting off her lines. They backed slowly out of the slip, swung downriver, and roared away like weekend playboys, their craft out of costume now, sailless, her phony mast laid back, flying over the water like a cigarette boat.

Karen was hurrying to the end of the dock to see which way they turned. "In case the police want to know."

"They are the police," Paul explained. They were heading south, toward the bay. He could finally bring himself to admit that he'd never see the fink Will again.

In the cabin Paul said he wanted me to have the *Sea Something*.

"Cover the slip rental, and she's yours till I come home." I was wild for the boat, though not at the cost of losing Paul. It was the first I'd heard of his Canadian exit. "What about Karen?"

"She's gone for the clippers. Don't worry," he said, "she wants you to have it, too." We indulged ourselves for the moment in a reverie of Canadian freedom, and Chesapeake roaming.

"It's easy," Paul said. "Take the bathtub out, and drop in the big Packard under Roy's tarp. You'll be eating crab cakes in St. Michael's. If you put a couple of thousand in the hull, she'll fetch Bermuda."

Fetch? It was the posh word of a yachtsman in whites, as out of place in Paul's mouth as truffles. This was the way most of Port McHair had begun their stationary, river lives—in self-deception, improbable repair, imaginary shakedown cruises to the Eastern Shore. I stood on top of the cabin, spread my hands, and repeated Will's last Marxist lesson.

"We erect our structure in the imagination before we erect it in reality."

Posing as Will posing as Marx wasn't funny anymore. I agreed to take over care of the *Sea Something*. It was easy to say yes; I could afford to keep the boat and my apartment as well. Karen came back with the electric clippers Cretia used on the dog, and buzzed Paul's head. She began to cry when she saw the result.

Montreal was his destination because that's where "the *Montrealer*" went—the sleeper out of Washington—though Paul wouldn't be in the Pullman car. He'd be sitting up all night with the proles. At four in the afternoon, he was no closer to cadging his fare. I spent the afternoon trying to change his mind, prating the obvious.

"They want you to run," I said, "so they'll have a real charge against you. Then you really can't go home again."

After two hours in the station with no one paying attention to us, he'd come to the same conclusion. But he wouldn't give up on Montreal. He was trying to distract himself from what used to be called "mean changes," trying to make something drastic happen in his life.

"What about your father's bond?"

"I've already told him. I'm jumping it."

"Was it method acting," he asked me, "what Daisy and Will were doing?"

In Daisy's case I thought it might just have been playing herself. But her exit had been masterful, and in retrospect, maybe necessary to their purpose. Will would need a little sympathy, and maybe awe for his commitment, to make sure Paul wouldn't disappoint him. As for his performance, all Will had to do was memorize his lines and follow the Party reputation for rote delivery.

Two young Canadian women with rucksacks for suitcases sat on our bench, one with a French accent, and the other with a Mont Tremblant patch on her sleeve. Paul was coy, turning to them only when offered a Chicklet. After that it went very quickly. The story behind his bald head. Their fascination. The advance of his fare to Montreal against one of their father's credit cards. A promise of patronage in Canada. Possible work, without papers, for an uncle who built houses around Toronto. And their affectionate company, I supposed, through the long night ahead in the sitter. Paul was on his way.

It doesn't happen this way anymore. There isn't the same trust. Sex lost its wild license; fear rules, and mistrust. With national motive stated and restated to fit the moment; protesters lose the plot. The city of masks is more brazen than ever in its posing. There's no bond among the young.

These weren't my words. They were Paul's. He never came home. He married one of the women who helped him across the Canadian border. When he writes, now thirty-five years later, it's in wonder that I could still live here.

I went back to the *Sea Something* that night to get the feel of what I'd inherited, and found Cretia sleeping in one of my bunks with her dog.

"Do you mind?" she said. "Raoul's angry. Don't worry, I'll turn my back."

The mutt growled softly.

"No," I told her. "I'll go back to my apartment."

"Oh, good." she said. "That's best."

When I returned the next evening after work Cretia was still there. She'd made up the same bunk with her own bedding, and moved in a small hamper in which she kept clothes, dirty and clean. There was water all over the floor around the tub hatch.

"No," I said.

We debated. Only a few weeks, she said. "You don't need it. Why do you want to be here, anyway? Do you have anything in writing?"

I had no ready answer. She told me what Karen had really said—that she didn't want me using their river pad for lady bait. When Cretia got abusive I came out on deck. There on the dock, and on the boats to either side of me, were most of the McHair residents, gathered and listening to our argument, waiting to see who'd get Paul's boat.

"Throw her in the river," Billy said.

The others weren't taking sides, though I thought Raoul, whose eyes were near closed, might be praying for Cretia's victory, for some space to himself. Bess and Webber were reunited, watching silently. All of them waiting for an answer to Cretia's resonating question, "Why do you want to be here?"

I left the eviction to Roy, and moved to the boat a few days later. I lived in the minimal quarters of the *Sea Something* for two years, with girlfriend and without. It was Raoul who stiffened my will to move on board. I didn't have to justify my presence to Cretia, or anyone else, he said, not even to myself. The reason had nothing to do with my communal credentials, with manifesto, declaration, or preamble, he explained, but could be found in the first few pages of *Moby-Dick*, the maritime call.

"'Nothing contents them but the extreme limit of the land . . . they come from lanes and alleys, streets and avenues . . . they must get just as nigh the water as they can without falling in.'" Or, as Raoul himself put it, "nature's first water bed was a hammock at sea."

If that were all of it, why was he sitting with me at the end of the pier, staring at the nighttime river and at the point of land where Daisy and her *Daisy Mao* had disappeared from view? And wondering whether credulity or acting skills had deserved most credit for our suspension of disbelief. The *Daisy Mao*, we supposed, would be having a makeover in some clandestine boathouse on the bay. Living on the water as we were was like a refusal to be part of the larger charade.

The triple-tiered ferry for the amusement park at Marshall Hall, lights ablaze, came round the point, and for several minutes the dark, silent river beyond us was transformed into a smooth boulevard of merriment. There was a band on board. The decks were teeming. We could see dancers, and drinkers hanging over the rails, their bottles and glasses twinkling like handheld stars, giving outline to the whole ship.

We heard a moody saxophone interrupt the Twist with An Old Fashioned Love Song. Like a twentieth-century masque, a thousand faces floated past on the backlit set. I was certain they were all pretending they were somewhere else, maybe on their way to Orchard Beach, or Asbury Park, or Coney Island, anywhere but in the shadows of the feigned city they were leaving behind them.

They were looking for a lonely figure,
one with a school-wide resentment.

7

The Head of Farnham Hall

There are no more life tenures. The old venerables are gone, the autocrats—Boyden of Deerfield, Wing of Madiera, Pulling of Millbrook; farther back, Peck of St. Mark's—and their sovereign kind in chapelled domains across New England and down the East Coast. Nowadays you were lucky if you lasted a few years in the madeover world of the eastern prep school.

Instructors hang around for years, but not headmasters. Faculty dissension turns into revolt, a student armed with due process becomes a legal adversary, political correctness is a tightrope on which the most careful performers can lose their balance. A friendly trustee turns coat, and sends you packing.

Those old men would have laughed if you said a student had bent a campus to his will or brought a headmaster to his knees. And after ten years on the job Dr. Helen (Nell) Custis was still the Head at Farnham Hall, still moving assuredly atop the school, suspending, dismissing, firing. She was cunning and manipulative, believing these traits were requirements for longevity in the job, and she was therefore unapologetic.

Nell's armor was the Farnham mission, the ideals she summoned insistently—the advantages of single sex education for young women, tolerance, diversity. Her talk was completely self-assured, and perhaps that's why her students had so little sympathy for the speech impediment, her trouble with *r*.

In New York City, where Nell did three years as Head of Miss Zartmann's Classes, the parents called her zaftig. On this favored Pennsylvania campus on the banks of the Susquehanna—three acres per child the viewbook says—they were more apt to call her full figured. Here, where a regular vigil—a monthly weigh-in—was kept against anorectic or bulimic tendency, she made it clear the proper model at the center should not be a nervous, twiggy thing, but a sturdy bracing timber.

"Gulls," she said, "a gwave cwisis has awisen."

You couldn't blame some of them for losing control. She looked something like a schoolgirl herself, with thick dark hair whose single curl bounced on her shoulders, while her dark-blue dress, sashed at the waist, gave tidy definition to firm round lines. To her own ear she had only said, "Girls, a grave crisis has arisen." She waited while tittering gave way to silence.

"Someone here has sent a death threat to Ariana Fiske," Nell told the assembly, "someone maybe who thinks it's funny, or someone who's very sick."

A girl whispered, "vewwy sick."

"We're going to find out who it is," she said.

Here, where some of the girls wear tee shirts that read Farnham Hall, Most Expensive Form of Contraception, any embarrassment may be exaggerated in the city paper, even carried on the national wires. Farnham's worst scandals and tragedies have been sown by satellite over the globe. And the thirty-year-old story of a headmaster's murder has an oral half-life stretching toward eternity.

Everyone snapped to full attention when the Head read the note that had been left in Ariana Fiske's book bag that morning:

"I'M GOING TO KILL YOU, BITCH. DIE."

It wasn't the first note to Ari. They'd been coming all week. There was one on her door the night before:

"GUESS WHO. AND DIE."

"Whoever you are," Nell said, "We want to help you."

—✣—

The trouble fell on the school a week after she'd fired the arts faculty, two studio teachers, and the photography instructor Russell Berry for no announced reasons. The remaining teachers hadn't time to let go of that grievance before they were dealing with this new problem. The county police came to ask questions, but the Head thought they weren't up to the challenge.

"We need experts," she told her A team, her crisis council—the Academic Dean Mr. Trubner and Ms. Robey, Chair of History. These two met with her in her office at the first sign of trouble, though they served as little more than supporting listeners and relay officers, making notes on policy as she announced it, and carrying the news to the rest of the school.

"We need more subtlety," she told them. And the next day she had a handwriting expert, a forensic man, and a psychologist visiting dorms and classrooms. And a technician installing a miniature surveillance camera on the wall opposite Ariana's room, as if the camera could be kept a secret.

At the next morning's assembly there were shadows of fear and pity on the girl's scrubbed faces. The thing was being wound to such a pitch, the threats seemed to call out for their fulfillment: "Show me you mean it!"

The girls' pity was for themselves and for Ariana, who as proctor in her dorm had set a strong example. Before she found the white powder in the Carter girl's room, hers was the corridor where the admissions office sent prospective girls and their families for a glimpse of the Farnham family at ease.

Perhaps the threats were just a bad joke, Dean Trubner suggested. And if so, wasn't the school's reaction excessive? But thirty years after Dr. Boyle's murder in the master bedroom of the Headmaster's residence—a murder never solved—Farnham still cringes at the first hint of scandal. Nell could say she was only guiding the school away from a possible charge of negligence.

She reminded a girl again of a favorite motto—"function in adversity, finish in style." Yet the curriculum was stopped in its tracks. Girls stood in line waiting to be fingerprinted, while others sat for a psychological testing. There could be no easy retreat after this. Too late to plead prank, Nell told her crisis council. The guilty one would be stewing in the momentum of her shame, and appropriate that the whole school—students and faculty—would be the trap that closed around the culprit. The affair could not drift away as a trifle.

Scornful as Nell was of the deputies' simplistic formulation: "A death threat is never a prank, it's always a crime," it was the one thing she took from them at face value. When they told her, "the victim in these cases is quite often the perpetrator," she reminded them of Ariana's record, a calm cruise toward most any college she might choose, her gentle nature, her field hockey skills. Ever so bright, and with it all, her selfless mentoring of the younger and less capable.

"She's never used profanity," Dean Trubner reminded them all.

One deputy rolled his eyes and the other tapped his foot. Nell excused herself from the meeting, telling them, "Look for yourselves." Ariana was helpless, hardly eating, trembling with fear.

Back in her office she opened a letter from the fired photography instructor, Russell Berry, a decent young man with a boyish shock of blond hair, a craggy face, and after seven years of service, perhaps too much admired by the Farnham girls for the wrong reasons. He wrote, "Several of my former associates tell me you say I left Farnham under a cloud. What cloud? You never mentioned a cloud. You told me you were 'restructuring' the art department."

With that his note turned into a lecture. "No one person can be the savior of Farnham Hall. The school is ninety years old. No Head, or board of trustees, or group of students can claim to be the school. It prevails across time. It will outlast your reign of terror. It will put you behind it."

Nell tore the page in half. Her tenure, treated as an unpleasant interlude, a poor fraction of a century, set her back only for a moment. She recovered and put the two halves of the letter in Berry's file in case the troublesome name should come her way again. Reign of terror? Ten years? How could anyone believe hers was a reign of terror? A reign, yes. To these shifting populations you were either a consistent disciplinarian or an appeasing failure. A benevolent reign, she was comfortable with that.

Nell believed Mr. Berry had flouted a clear rule: any untoward communication from a student to faculty member must be reported immediately to the office of the Head. For the teachers' protection as well as the girls'. It was her information that Berry had dallied with a mash note from one of the girls, even described it to another instructor, perhaps boasted about it. She had not accused him because she couldn't prove it. In any case, she never felt he was on her team. She didn't have to tell anyone why she fired him.

In the third assembly since announcement of the death threats one of her problem children, Claudia Hempel, rose and turned to Ariana.

"This is so unfair to you," she said.

Claudia was a solitary spirit, unafraid of censure. A senior, she had taken the school's feminist baton and run with it at a speed that left others winded and scornful. "I am large growing larger," she wrote in lit. mag. poesy, putting all on notice she was not only tall but adding girth, month by month.

Nell had heard lots more about Claudia. For example, after her mandatory weigh-ins, the school nurse said Claudia called out the news, as if each new pound supported her indifference to fashion. And she gave the figure in stones, not because it made a dainty number; rather it furthered her claim that she was an English girl cruelly transplanted to a home in Grafton, Indiana. From her calculus teacher Nell learned that Claudia crossed her sevens at the blackboard while the other girls groaned at another English affectation.

Claudia turned to the Head.

"And it's unfair to us. We're all behind you, Ari."

Nell could imagine this one coming back in twenty years, addressing the same hall as the moral soul of a cause too compelling for anyone to scorn. She was a misfit now, too willing to flaunt her peculiarity. Her name was being repeated by the investigators as a child of interest, a suspect, and Nell had no reason to doubt it.

Classes were on normal schedule again. The cyclic chores of the school continued. The seniors had to study their way through this dark month into the white gowns of graduation, and an underclass had to be recruited to share a happier season. Now came the mother of a prospective freshman to the Head office to explain her dilemma. "The dormitories of the Cranston School aren't fit for my daughter, and the Farnham stables aren't fit for my daughter's horse."

The document examiner said, "left-handed capitals." Little help that was. But all the girls in Pritcher Dormitory reproduced the note with their left hands:

MAYBE I'LL HAVE MY BROTHER KILL YOU

The drama director thought this one, which was left in Ariana's book bag, might have been influenced by the fall production of *The Libation Bearers*. And a bloody spectacle it was, though the girls in the audience had been more impressed by the actors' feats of memory than the slaughter. All those turgid lines of Aeschylus! Claudia was the cue master; she memorized the whole thing. On opening night even the Chorus needed prompting: "When the blood of slaughter wets the ground, it wants more blood."

In the second week of the investigation Nell's technical hires were making little progress. They seemed stuck on the one name, Claudia, but with no proof. The camera opposite Ariana's door was an open secret, and the Grayson twins turned their bare rumps to its lens. Comic relief, Nell supposed, from the clutch of real fear. None of the girls in single rooms were sleeping alone.

Parents were calling their children home. Four had gone. The soft-spoken Mr. Seldon, the forensic psychiatrist, was still on the case, testing, interviewing, developing profiles. The pattern, he said, was a common one, an acceleration of recklessness, increasing frequency of threats, a promise of violence. A rushing to be caught, he said.

YOU'RE GOING TO WAKE UP WITH
MY KNIFE IN YOU, BITCH

They were looking for a girl with a schoolwide resentment, Seldon said. And he was all but certain they'd found her. The obvious Claudia Hempel. She was far too quick, he thought, to speak in that early assembly. While others were still dumbstruck, it was Claudia who had assimilated the thing, and was promising a solution.

Out of her two hundred eighty Nell thought Seldon might have chosen someone more private and devious, someone who had sacrificed less of her popularity to principle. She didn't really care for Seldon. Short and thin, hunched shoulders, arms glued to his sides, he was a small man trying to be smaller. Self-effacing, the kind who believe that if their egos disappear, their arguments carry more weight. He was almost whispering, "Claudia presents as an angry outcast from two societies, from the world at large, and from her school. She wears her lesbianism not as a comfortable cloak as one might hope for her, but as a suit of armor."

And how, Nell wondered, would she herself "present" to this wisp of a rationalist? As a divorced woman with masked anger, scorned by the ex-husband perhaps, with two grown children and a speech impediment? A woman whose compensating pathology was autocratic control of a school? A woman who surrendered too often perhaps to a rich dessert to demonstrate her right to the indulgence?

"The child shows a sour profile," Seldon told her. "Confrontational posing. There was a time one might have said she was an ectomorph in an endomorph's body. Behaving like Cassius but looking like Falstaff. Of course those terms are largely discredited."

The more they probed, the more Claudia's imposing silhouette was coaxed into menacing relief. Her routine fit so neatly, and her dorm room was close to the victim's. She knew the details of Ariana's schedule. And Claudia spent many hours alone, which allowed her clandestine movement. She knew where Ariana kept her toothbrush: in the lavatory, hidden on the water tank over a commode. That's where the victim found a final note that brought the Greek tragedy home.

PRITCHER IS THE HOUSE OF ATREUS
AND YOU'RE THE HOUSE MOTHER

This sent the investigators to their Aeschylus, where they made a simple translation: Ariana is Clytemnestra, due for death, and Claudia Hempel's profile was large and growing larger. With the threat taking a scholarly turn, Nell asked if they should be looking for a second criminal. The idea was put to rest. The tone of the notes was of no consequence, Seldon told her, since it was all a kind of posing. What mattered, he said, was this acceleration into a psychotic danger zone.

"I can't dismiss a child on mere speculation," Nell protested to no one in particular. And no one on her crisis team answered. The solution came to her as a gift of their silence.

"We'll put her in the infirmary for a while."

"I think she's quite a sick girl," Seldon agreed.

Nell was already on to the next questions. What do we tell her parents? Do we allow visitors in to see Claudia?

Nobody home at the Grafton, Indiana, residence. An answering machine gave an international code and number. A moment more and Nell was connected to a hotel in one of the Arab Emirates. And her voice knocked into Mr. Hempel's, circling half the globe.

"We're terribly worried about Claudia," she began.

It went more easily than she could have hoped. Mr. Hempel wasn't surprised that Claudia was in trouble, considering the sort of things her mother, now in California, had allowed. He could not be home for another week. The school would have to keep her until then.

"Of course," Nell agreed. "We want to keep her apart for a while."

"I blame her mother," Mr. Hempel said, for a second time.

Would Claudia be going to England again this summer? Nell asked.

"That again? She's never been to England in her life." He couldn't stay on the line any longer.

Nell might have reached out now to the confused child who had wrapped herself in an elaborate and fictitious English childhood. But a pride of seniors coming across the common, the plucky Ariana among them, brought her back to duty, and a chance to prove she knew their names.

Nell never had a problem bringing girls to heel. They followed, they obeyed, or they were gone. The majority were docile enough. The more difficult ones might pose as tough or diffident, but in the confines of Nell's office they were outfaced and usually broke down. It could be pathetic the way their voices cracked and faltered.

She ordered a winter bouquet for the vase beside her office sofa. It was actually more like a love seat than an interrogation bench. Claudia could not settle her bulky length comfortably on its soft upholstery. She leaned back against the sofa's arm, raised a foot onto the cushions, and let the other dangle.

"Please relax."

Claudia was doing more than that, cocking her head, appraising, taking in the room's appointments, smoothing the sofa's nap, touching the flowers.

"I have an English friend," she said, "whose mother had a tulip named for her."

Perhaps if the girl had been given a part in the fall, Nell thought, perhaps if she'd been allowed to do her Aeschylus on the stage. The girl wore no makeup. Her clothes sagged over the floppy terrain of her large bosom and belly. Her whole being cried out to the school, You tricked-out posers, my beauty is all inside, where it belongs.

Nell began. "You haven't been very happy here, have you?"

"I left my real friends in England," she said.

"So I'm right. You haven't been very happy."

Claudia picked at her front teeth with a fingernail, and began slowly. "You know what my mother says about that? She says, 'show me a happy teenager, and I'll show you a screwed up adult.'"

"Claudia, we think there may be a connection between the Drama Club and the trouble we're having."

"Sure. The Aeschylus stuff."

"But beyond that. Maybe somebody in the club, and not very happy with the role she has there."

Claudia sat forward, suddenly filling the space between them. Her foot tapped the floor.

"Do you know what Nietzsche said about these Greek tragedies, Claudia?"

"No."

The foot drummed faster and a hand went to her mouth.

"He said, 'All that exists is just and unjust, and equally justified in both.'"

Claudia's lip began to tremble.

"What do you think he meant by that?" Nell asked her.

"I don't know. Maybe there's no use moralizing about revenge, because it has a morality of its own."

"Is that what you think, Claudia? Is that what justifies you?"

"Me?" Her eyes darted about for an escape that only her wits could provide.

"Revenge for what in this case?" Nell pressed.

Claudia wanted to say something, but couldn't because she was sobbing. She raised her shaking hands, pointed to her chest in a grand gesture of disbelief. And for the first time she raised her voice.

"You're as stupid as the others! Just like that little man! You can't find who did it so you blame me!"

"I haven't blamed you."

Just as Nell had hoped, the thing was resolving itself. The girl's crying protest that they'd all be sorry, she wasn't finished with them, was as close to confession as she got. Claudia broke down completely as the confinement was explained to her. Visitors, yes. But she could not come out of the infirmary. Meals would be carried to her from the dining room. She should try to make the best of it. Catch up with her work.

Not the end of the world. The school doctor came over from Montour to sedate her. Campus security watched the door. And the news passed dorm to dorm; Claudia's in the infirmary, no knife allowed on her tray.

Nell watched and waited as the school corrected course. In a couple of days the girls were sleeping more easily, and going about their lavatory routines without insisting on a partner. A third day passed, and Mrs. Rosenman, kind lady of Romance language, for whom Latin had never died, and who'd been the vade mecum—the go with me—of many a broken spirit in her long career, visited with Claudia and came out with a report that a calmness had settled over the child. Remarkably she was smiling, possessed by a secret happiness.

Nell was thankful the school had a Mrs. Rosenman, someone to pillow the whimpering of the coming dismissal. And she was pleased to hear that Claudia had let the school nurse wash her hair, found radiant as a bay horse under the gray film. For this concession the nurse played chess with the prisoner, and carelessly Claudia gave her inexperienced opponent's pieces the names of her classmates as she removed them from the battlefield. Sometimes the opposing Queen was Ariana, sometimes Dr. Nell Custis.

As Claudia walked further into their trap, Seldon said it would be dishonest to remain at the school any longer on his per-diem rate. He and his colleagues rose in Nell's office. Their briefcases snapping shut were much louder than their voices.

There were two more quiet and healing days. Mr. Hempel arrived to gather his daughter into his disappointed arms, and to discuss a surrender to circum-

stance. The school must be prudent and the family re-
alistic. They must understand, Nell agreed that no legal
scale had weights fine enough to balance the rights of
the school with those of the Hempels. In return for
Claudia's departure the school would confer an early
diploma. Claudia and her father were on a plane to Indiana.

Icy cold and crystal clear. It was a morning of new begin-
nings for the survivors above the Susquehanna. No need
to remind her girls they were the privileged few. In the
morning inspirational Nell asked them to be assertive
and confident in their academic traces. They could prove
to the departed child and the world that the happy
young were not destined to a melancholy maturity.

Later that day, an "Oh, Jeeesus!" more moaned than
shouted was heard through the Head's office window.
Claudia Hempel hardly gone forty-eight hours and
here's another note in the Fiske girl's room. A small yellow sheet from a post-it pad, and another capital scrawl:
STILL HERE. LOOK OUT, BITCH!

They didn't need to summon the experts or call the
County police. Within an hour Ariana confessed to
writing all the poison to herself. More matter of fact
than emotional or contrite in recounting her month of
damage, she even asked Nell to explain to her why
she'd done it.

And Nell had a name for it, "the perfect child syndrome."

It was a rationale for those who crack after years of performing to high expectation without deviation, as if an excuse might begin to repair what had happened or was wanted at a time like this, when punishment and penance knocked so clearly at the Farnham gate.

Alone above her school, betrayed by the little man's flimsy social science, Nell prepared herself for the morning assembly in which she explained the awful mistake to her disbelieving girls.

"We act," she said, "on the best information we have at the time." Her apology canceled by self-justification condemned the girl all over again. By that evening Nell was on a plane to Indiana, dispatched by her board with a portfolio of whatever it might take—anything— to mollify, to cut their losses.

Next morning in a rental she drove through a farm-squared landscape, where trees seemed never to be sheltering, always on the horizon. Here, where God lived on roadside crosses and cautionary billboards, she was made more aware of the tentative faith she taught by default, that salvation might be found in the searching academic soul.

Heart full, she stood in the door of a Victorian on Grafton's only avenue, and made her humble greeting to father and daughter.

"We owe you so much. We want her back."

She had not rehearsed the simple lines, or emotional honesty would not have run so wildly ahead of caution.

Mr. Hempel nodded. She asked herself across the threshold and followed back into his little office, where computers and the electronic font from anywhere connected him to all the information a petroleum consultant might need. Though none of the machines, he said, could compute the damage the Farnham School had done to his daughter.

Nell felt her eyes fill.

"Perhaps, Claudia, you'll let your father and me speak alone."

"No!" he said.

Could the family ever forgive the school? Would it give Claudia back to walk with her graduating class? In the father's silence Nell understood he was reaching through her remorse, past the abject questions, toward a settlement on his daughter's injuries. The Farnham endowment was at risk on Nell's watch.

She had in mind a grand mea culpa, an assembly devoted to nothing but this tragic mistake, a meeting from which Claudia could emerge completely vindicated. She began to describe a healing process in which the whole school would participate. Mr. Hempel interrupted.

"We've had no legal advice."

A muscle in Nell's cheek did an unbidden dance and her fingers tightened on the arm of her chair "We're prepared . . . "

"I think we'd have a year to make a claim."

He was thinking aloud in increments of damage "Five days as a prisoner in your infirmary . . . the libe implied . . . the whole school invited to pick at her rep utation . . . the expense of treating her emotiona health . . . for who knows how long . . . you stuck her with a needle, didn't you, as if she were a mental pa tient."

"I want to go back," Claudia said.

"Good, good," Nell encouraged her. "Then you'l walk with your class."

"But you've already graduated her," Mr. Hempel re minded her. "You'll have to waive the rest of her tu ition."

All this and more, Nell promised, as the need migh occur to the family.

Claudia was welcomed back to Farnham in the prom ised redemptive assembly. The girls cheered for thei martyr a little too long, Nell thought, perhaps too rau cously, in a way that could only be heard as a reproach to herself. Now that she was back it seemed unnatura that Claudia would want to be there, that the calm fac she wore must mask some motive of which even sh might be unaware.

Nell saw that the ordeal had taken weight off the girl, and lightened her step. Claudia was doing her hair with a curl at the shoulder, like the Head's, and wore a similar wide felt ribbon over the top. Her new attention to appearance included use of a bra, which she justified not as political, but simply good manners.

Nell called her in to bury the past, and was surprised to see Claudia in dark skirt and white blouse, very much like her own. She saw no guile in this, no presumption, rather an admiring imitation.

"Trying out for the spring play?"

"There won't be time." Claudia said she was going to be monitoring several classes, not actually taking them, not taking tests or anything like that. "I'll be doing a lot of outside reading. Novels and stuff."

Some of this would have to be set right, Nell thought, but not just yet. She'd give her space and do nothing to upset her.

"I'm doing some of the A.P. courses they wouldn't let me in before. And Mr. Parker's senior seminar on Joyce and Yeats. You know how he always goes right to the sexuality of a book? I'm going to keep an eye on that for you . . . and—" she interrupted herself. "You know that thing you have?"

"Thing?"

"The way you talk? Until my brother was fifteen he was a tongue thruster too. It can be corrected."

If Nell was dealing with a new and awkward daughter, the rest of the school, too, was put back on its heels. The mass apology and the balance of the other girls' forbearance for their mistreated sister was rapidly being drawn down.

Claudia's fresh approach to Farnham included regular announcements at the morning assembly, usually following Nell's inspirational with some amendment to the Head's presentation, along with advice of her own. Of course the girls still talked more about her than to her, but Claudia didn't seem to care. With her British affectation, she seemed more self-assured than ever.

As winter deepened, she popped into Nell's office with annoying regularity. In an assembly in early January she came forward after the Head's talk about the honor code to second the argument and go it one better.

"Dr. Custis is right about the cheating. But we have to remember the school can be undermined by suspicion."

Turning to Nell, sitting behind her on the podium, she said, "I think we'd be better off letting some of these accusations evaporate in the gossipy air, don't you?"

Nell bit her tongue. None of this seemed plausible, yet it was happening to her. Mr. Hempel called every week to make sure his daughter's path to June was smooth. The morning microphone could not be denied her. She was making herself the Head's double, and as the school's roving defender, she was bidding to turn Nell into the lesser, if not the evil, twin.

As February melted into March on the Susquehanna moor, the groundsmen set out the boardwalks between buildings that kept the girls' feet out of the mud. Nell's flock, beset with sniffles and inward pity, needed reminding of their conceits, their privilege, and the effort spent on their comfort.

In her office she jotted, "Raised from mire by faithful service of others. Remember others." But now she had to think two moves ahead of her young shadow; the lives of the ground crew are no less significant than our own? No, that wasn't quite it. Her thinking took to the air, where Claudia might not be prepared to follow. "You're not weightless, as astronauts in orbit—though nothing need stop you from becoming astronauts. As gravity holds us to earthly routine, so . . . "

Just a few notes to ease her through the morning talk without rebuttal. She'd advise them to keep down to earth, and pull harder in their scholar's harness . . ." No, no. Deserted by inspiration, she turned to a late flurry of parental anxiety pent behind the cycling lights on her phone.

"Is there a girl coming and going as she pleases? Driving her own car into town?"

"My daughter says the Hempel child takes no exams."

"Were you aware that Claudia Hempel sleeps here and there, in one dorm and another? My daughter is very upset. Are there no rules about this?"

And from Ms. Esty, the college counselor, waiting on Nell's desk for her initials was Farnham's college recommendation for Claudia, as emended yet again by her father, with deletions and insertions. *Stood out* replaced *held her own. A natural leader* filled the hole where *singular personality* was crossed out. The two pages were full of changes.

Nell looked up to the office ceiling. A little water damage and a few cracks were no help. She attached a note—"Can we live with this?"—hoping to keep Dean Trubner out of it this time. She didn't want his bullying support, but here he was again in her office, his timing too perfect to be chance. And Ms. Esty right behind him.

"Every family has a right to see their daughter's transcript and our recommendation," Trubner argued.

"To see. Not to edit," Ms. Esty shot back.

"The right to view presumes the right to contest." He backed away, looking to Nell for confirmation.

"To contest matters of fact, not opinion," Ms. Esty had the last word.

And the room, like the school at large, fell silent again, waiting for the Head to speak.

Her morning inspirational was almost over.

"And as you consider the weightless astronauts, as you consider gravity and the truths of space travel . . . "

This was too much for a cabal of juniors, whose laughter broke through their cupped hands and moved along the back row. The disturbance came forward, sideways and forward again, grew to a critical saturation, and burst through the whole auditorium. Even some of the faculty couldn't help themselves. Somewhere in back, a whispered "gwavity and the twooths of space twavel" had set them off.

On the verge of rebuking them, Nell felt something fall away. The blush of reflexive anger moved from her scalp and down her cheeks; she sensed the red demarcation receding across her neck and disappearing. Standing back, she joined in the fun, laughing at herself.

It was enough to recapture the room—all but Claudia Hempel, who was standing, approaching the podium. There, turned out like a larger Nell, she pulled the microphone to her mouth with the practiced flip of the Head.

"Actually," she said, "astronauts at orbiting altitude retain ninety-five percent of their attraction for the earth. They only think they're weightless because the world falls away from them at the same speed they fall toward it. Relativity." As if that word alone would get everyone thinking clearly.

There was no relief. In the best light, Nell might have taken the change in Claudia as a deserved and welcome renaissance. She could hardly admit she was holding on for the moment the legal shadow would pass beyond them, sometime in the following December, if the trustees' counsel had it right, six months after Claudia would be gone from Farnham.

As the final semester wore on, Nell was less inclined to deliver uplift. Sessions in her office were chosen at Claudia's whim. Though they might be delayed, they couldn't be denied altogether without risking one of the father's legal adumbrations—"Claudia seems depressed this week." And so it went toward June with the girl's presence ever more intrusive.

"I don't have time now, dear," she told Claudia.

"I'll only take a moment. I'm thinking it's all very well to take seed and inseminate ourselves, but what if the child is male? Should we love him less? Do we deny him sexual freedom? I don't think so."

Claudia was tapping softly on Nell's desk, insisting on her attention. "What I mean is, I know we're different, you and I, but let's not get rid of all the male teachers. I mean like Mr. Berry. I'm sorry about what happened to him."

"I can't talk about that, Claudia. Why should you be sorry?"

"Something else. I think you should remind everyone that we're born with our sexual preference. I mean, after all, you're a lesbian too, aren't you?"

"No. I'm not. You know I was married. I have two children."

Claudia threw back her head at such a discredited piece of evidence.

"Anyway," she said, "I wanted you to see this." And she went off, for some free time in the library.

Nell, thinking she'd gotten to the root of the girl's importunate advice and imitation, unfolded the piece of loose-leaf paper. A note from Claudia to Mr. Berry.

Dear Mr. Berry,

Thank you for talking to me. You're the only teacher who does. I mean about things that aren't school stuff. You're the only one in the whole school I'd share my self with, even if you are a man. Remember when we were freshmen you had us make pinhole cameras out of oatmeal boxes? We had to do a series of pictures with them? I called mine "Sand Dunes." Did you know they weren't sand dunes, they were all pictures of me? If you had put them together you could have seen all of me. Were you embarrassed? I hope not. I know you're supposed to tell when you get a letter like this. I'm trusting you to tear it up or give it back to me.

Claudia

Again Nell looked to her ceiling, to the cracks and spreading water stain. No answer there but decay and change. In the mail on her desk was a letter from her board chairman—appreciation for her steady hand on the helm through the school's stormy weather. Then a heads up for an item the board was adding to the next meeting's agenda: long-term leadership goals.

Already, she could sense them putting distance between themselves and their drifting Head. When she considered how she'd suffer Claudia all the way to June, chat by chat, it never occurred to her that a correspondence might last beyond graduation.

Hotel Russell
Russell Square
London

Dear Dr. Custis,

Is it time for me to start calling you Nell? My trip to the British Isles is a smashing success. My thanks to you and Farnham for underwriting educational travel, something I could never get my father to do. Ireland, Wales and Scotland are all lovely to look at. My mother says, you can't live in pubs and inns forever. At last I'm in England again where people are so out of date. It's wonderful! I think of you sharing this with us.

Yes, I've made a great friend here. She'll be going with me to Greece, and I have to say thanks to Farnham again.

Nell was negotiating with a country day school outside of Austin, and more than a little progressive in its own community. Coeducational. She could deal with that; the teachers took sensitivity training for gender equity. And they were onto something neoclassic, public speaking across the curriculum required all four years. How such a place would react to a soft *r* never entered her mind.

A final postcard from Claudia toward the end of the summer holiday was forwarded to Texas.

Greetings from Thira,

Neither Jenny nor I can imagine the Aegean as the harbor of classic vengeance. The walls are blinding white in the sun, the sky is crystalline, and the sea actually is "wine dark." Do you remember the line from Aeschylus? "Both fists at once come down. Zeus crushes their heads." Not here. Impossible.

Remember my second scramble
up the rungs?

8

The Shape of the Past

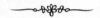

To say the retired widower Walter Paige loved his home was as unnecessary, in a local way, as declaring to the Aegean region the unyielding affection of Menelaus for Helen. To call Paige house proud, as his wife used to do, was to strike a nerve. It was his secret and scarcely qualified blessing (he now foraged, cooked, and cleaned for himself) that she was no longer here on earth to pick at the core of his vanity, the house at 28 Maple, Collins Ford, Virginia.

In fact Walter was vain of little other than his well-preserved home, save for the endearments he'd gathered merely by offering a civil manner to his neighbors for an adult lifetime on the same village block, the recognition of his face, and the expectation of his good-will. He was not proud of his career in the freight office in Brunswick, nor his long submission to a difficult marriage, nor the lack of courage in his infidelities (only one of them ever carried beyond his imagination), nor his thin sheaf of poetry, worked and overworked to desiccation, much less his collection of fifty-three arrowheads, though some men look to the ground all their lives and never find one.

He had the house painted every four years, not because it was needed. Rather, he imagined the wood-framed residence accreting armor, coat by coat, against future weathering, against a time when someone who knew no better would begin to let things slide—that is, when he, childless, would die and someone beyond blood would take ownership of the place he considered a family heirloom. There was no deferred maintenance at 28 Maple.

His siding glittered in the sun, every facet multiple-coated to a shiny patina. And every roof slate was firmly in place. The flashing, gutters, and downspouts were copper and apparently eternal. Built between the world wars by his great uncle, Harris Paige, when rough-cut heart pine was still used for framing, the house sat in the line of Victorian beauties known as dogwood row, beyond view of the sprawl at the eastern end of the village.

In breezy, insulting real estate parlance it was a Castle Victorian—as if there were comparables—owing to the round cone-roofed tower at its northwest corner, fit with custom-milled curved sash and curved glass. The tower jutted into a wraparound porch decorated with plentiful gingerbread and dowel work, the kind of detail that drove a housepainter beyond the day's fumes into a bar.

Of course he was pleased with his home, pleased and proud. He admired the soundproof plaster walls, the doors that brushed the jambs just so, wet season or dry; the carved pattern in the chair railing, the hand-planed beading on the trim. He liked the gentle knocking of the pipes that fed heat from a basement oil burner, calming as a cricket; the radiators and the little keys that turned their water cocks to bleed them at the change of seasons.

That was another of the tasks that had stupefied his wife, driving her discontent. He refused to refit the house with double-hung glass. She had none of his sentiment for the heavy, smooth-sliding, counterweighted windows, which responded to the touch of a finger and sat obediently in place till they were touched again. A little drafty, but wasn't fresh air the point?

Twenty-eight Maple was one of the two dozen houses the artisan Harris Paige had built in Collins County, four of them right there on dogwood row. Walter, familiar in and out with all four, was sure his own was the finest. It had annoyed his wife that he boasted of it, even as others had their oil burners torn out and heat pumps installed during the fashionable insulating madness of the seventies. You couldn't break wind in those homes, he maintained, without the lingering evidence to remind you of your pious economy.

For all these reasons he kept a favorite line of Andrew Marvell to himself, "Two Paradises 'twere in one, To live in Paradise alone." These should have been the years he could slide backward toward the grave in peace. He'd hoped he would die here in his bed before some busybody carted him off to assisted living.

On a daily descent into his basement, which was divided into laundry, shop, and the cook's room of another era, he stopped in the shop to open Harris Paige's tool chest, age-worn with the little darkened scars of a career Walter thought more honorable than his own. It was filled with the same wooden-handled tools that built the house, four layers of compartments and neat rows. He marveled at the seven graded gimlets. Standing over the retired tools he mumbled, "all trades, their gear and tackle and trim."

Then into the cook's sitter, where Delores Patischall and her two children had taken refuge for a season after their house burned down. At first he'd been against the intrusion, didn't want two little monkeys mucking around the house, getting into things, or anyone penetrating the proud walls surrounding the testy noise of his marriage. By the end of the visitors' stay it was Mrs. Paige who wanted them out.

All these years later the good turn has been turned again, turned on its head. After touring his basement, sniffing at the past, at a musty bedcover, and running his fingers over the bare hangers of a closet that was only a curtain hung in front of a pole, he went back up the stairs to his desk, took up pen and paper, and began to write.

Deirdre, against the objections of my lawyer I'll tell you what I remember, before history is stretched, under oath, beyond recognition. Lawyer be damned. You refuse to speak to me, and send your ultimatum in writing. How else can I reply but in writing?

I have no allies in this. My lawyer is so clearly your enemy, he can't possibly represent *me*. In my mind I'm still your admiring friend Walter Paige. The one who gave you the second name, "Druid." Not quite an anagram for your too-perfumed Deirdre, but inspired by your wild red hair and all the hours you spent in your tree house.

Before I go further, I'll tell you that one of your recovered-memory experts, the one who called himself a facilitator, has tried to break me down, calling my arguments obvious. He says they're full of smug precision, just what he'd expect in the posturing of a guilty conscience. So let me ask you, if you were an old man accused of this stuff, how would you react? Wouldn't you be defensive?

Of course, I'm referring to that season thirty years ago, when you were eleven and your brother Martin, seven. It's hard to believe that I was only forty-six then, though already ancient in a child's estimation. It was the summer your house burned to the ground, and your family made me a hero far beyond the reach of the *Collins Ford Sentinel*.

Actually, my deeds were ordinary and partly selfish. First, selling your mother the homeowner's policy in the nick of time. And, a week later, arriving at Martin's window with my extension ladder before we heard sirens. Do you remember my second scramble up the rungs for your cat, whose fear exploded in claws and excrement on my shoulder?

The very same night my wife—your brother Martin called her Mistuss Paige—insisted that your mother bring you and Martin to stay with us next door to your disaster until the house could be rebuilt. How could your mother refuse? A widow of few means beyond her teacher's salary at the Christian Academy. But I see in the social worker's report that "Mr. Paige invited Dolores Patischall and her children . . ." as if even then I was angling for proximity to you.

Within the year, we were paid stars of a television commercial. Our whole story, or so we thought—fire, rescue and compensation—pressed into a minute to glorify the insurance company. But wait till they get hold of this. It's what they love, a hero reduced to a beast. It won't be passed over. Not now, when the darkest private sensation sells the soap. You can be sure they'll ask Martin to appear on one of the afternoon confessionals after the courts are finished with us.

You want to know why you should trust an old man's memory, even if you were disposed to. It's a hoary truth that at seventy-six one can remember more about what happened on a day thirty years ago than what he did last Tuesday. Yet you can be sure our warring lawyers, no matter what instruction we give them, will defile that year when your family became part of mine, when water became almost as thick as blood.

You'll be laid out flat, a pre-teen jezebel. I'll be an old goat, and worse. Perhaps Martin will be drawn as a child arsonist, and experts will be called to explain his transferred guilt. Your mother's name, absent from the complaint, will be paired with "unfit," and "negligent." But I see her then as guileless if impatient, setting off for the Christian Academy each morning on her bicycle, her hair flying out behind, a red flag of warning to motorists that she could not be intimidated.

In her diminished family your mother was caught between duty to your father's memory—the votive candles that proved so dangerous—and a temptation to find a new life for herself. Though Martin was four years your junior, the two of you seemed to act at times with a kinship beyond blood. Like twins perhaps, the way your eyes and bodies would shift together at good news or a reprimand. It shouldn't surprise me that thirty years later you'd act in unison again, magnifying one of these recovered memories through a common lens.

You came into our house as guests. It might have been kinder to charge a nominal rent to relieve your mother's sense of obligation. Too fine a point for my wife, who said, "Delores can't afford it, and I won't accept it." The three of you had to share our basement room. We put down small rugs to keep your feet off the cold cement floor. There was a sink with hot and cold water. Dolores sent you upstairs for toilet duty and major washing up. I can hear Martin calling:

"Is it free yet?"

You were so embarrassed for him. The bathroom was bound to be a point of friction, though really the arrangement worked well enough with a rule for the seat—"down when leaving"—and a schedule. Mrs. Paige and I had first use in the morning and last in the evening.

Your reduced circumstances made you impudent rather than grateful. It was a shock to your pride to be sent to bed underground after second-story life in your own house. You had a mind for some kind of revenge, but still I expected you to look me in the eye when we spoke, to have you and Martin accept my appreciation of your hardship with some respect.

At the start you scurried around beneath us on your spindly legs, instructing your brother in petty rebellion.

You showed him how to plug the sink and run the water till it spilled over. You had some nerve; you wouldn't desert him when the blame came down. But no, I never told your mother her children were disrespectful. She came to that conclusion on her own. When you learned there were people in Collins Ford who called me Choo Choo, you taught Martin to toot like a train and go choo-chooing through the house when the women were out shopping. But it wasn't I who banished you to the basement. That, too, was Delores. She was afraid Mrs. Paige would ask her to leave.

Who was I at forty-six? I don't think my lawyer has decided yet. Whether he'll have me spent, sexless and forced into early retirement from the freight office, or reinvented as a vigorous, contented man in a marriage that had already reached silver, so fulfilled in his work that he'd undertaken a second career, selling fire policies to families such as your own. Either way, short of truth.

I'd been let go at the railroad. Not for drinking, as our choo-chooing neighbors had it, but for using the suggestion box unwisely. After fifteen years of docile duty, I vented steam for one season. My ideas were obvious, already in the manual, and therefore embarrassing. For example, if a box was to be checked through multiple depots, shouldn't routing be visible on its outside? All my suggestions came back from Baltimore with: "Well advised," which might as well have been corporate doublespeak for "Fire him."

Mrs. Paige was briefly satisfied with the idea of my selling insurance, and an office in our home where she could monitor my sales pitch and phone manners. Do you remember her face with the dimple that sucked on her cheek at a good joke? And the way she kept after herself with home permanents and the occasional diet book.

The enhancement was all in service to something that floated beyond her reach. Certainly beyond our home. No ardor between us. When we were young, a bed little larger than a cot was sufficient boundary to a night. By the time you moved in with us the spread wings of our mutual indifference couldn't be contained by a king-size mattress. This would not have impressed you since, like most children, you would have thought a sexual habit for the middle-aged beneath dignity, or at best, bizarre.

In the first transcript your people provided us, the state's investigator asks Martin, "Were you ever interfered with?" Who could fault your brother for repeating the question? One would suppose the rephrasing by the psychiatric social worker clarified everything:

"Were you ever touched inappropriately?"

Martin answered, "Yes."

"Where?"

"In his car."

"No. Where on your body did Mr. Paige touch you?"

"Well, you know, on the thing. He was driving me to school."

I think I know what he's referring to. I'll tell you what happened that morning. Martin had walked the half mile home from school immediately after arriving there on the bus. A remarkable hooky for a second-grader. Today it's called school refusal, another modern disease, just as daydreaming has a new name—attention deficit. Delores, late for work, accepted my offer to drive him back. She pushed him into my back seat and, seeing that his shoelaces were not tied, shirt out of his pants, etc., asked if I would do him up before delivering him to his teacher.

When we arrived at the school, Martin had done nothing to ready himself. I told him to tidy up and do up his fly, among other things. He couldn't, he said, the buttons were too large for their stiff and shrunken holes. I reached back over the seat, and helped him. A little struggle of awkward innocence, now turned loathsome by the behavior specialists.

As I understand it, Martin's recent discovery of his abuse came during counseling for a depression that keeps him almost housebound. But the therapist had his nugget and the search was on for the incriminating habits of a dirty old man. Several more hours of digging in one place—my house—and your brother claimed to recall your head next to mine on a blue pillow. And blue *was* the linen color preferred by Mrs. Paige in our bedroom.

So Martin came to you a month ago with his shocker: "Did you know we were both abused by Mr. Paige the year we came to live with him?" And you, too, submitted to psychic archeology until your "maybe," became "possibly," and then, "Yes, I can see myself next to him on the bed." From there, only a short step for the inquisitors to have you undressed beside me. And here in the record my name changes from Mr. Paige to "perpetrator."

You say that charges will be dropped if I confess, move from the community, and accept therapy. That your first concern is your mother, still my next-door neighbor, who must cringe to think our yards have been touching all these years, that our clotheslines have been hung with intimate semaphores of bed linen, shorts, lingerie.

When you came to us I thought we might have taken in a family of religious zealots. I was wrong. The candles were no sacrament. They were Martin's idea. If a president could have an eternal flame, why not your father? And Delores had little patience for her righteous colleagues in the Christian Academy. That should have been obvious since neither you nor Martin went there, though your tuitions would have been waived.

Not that your mother had no faith. "There are two bibles," she used to say. "One written by men and one by God. So which do you think is fallible?" She took that subversive question into her classroom each day, but asked it with enough subtlety to avoid the sack.

Children started at the Academy in the Fire Escape Pre-School on the second floor, accessed by an outdoor stairway. Delores called it the Avoid-the-Flames Kindergarten, where hell made its first appearance in the curriculum. A concept, she told us, that two knuckle-rapping women known as the first shepherds made corporeal.

Your clever mother put the required instruction to her own use. She turned the Moral Life hour she had to teach into occasional lessons in earth science. I remember, in particular, the way she explained *transubstantiation*, how she stripped the word of religiosity and applied it to fossils. "Repeat after me: Original hard material may be replaced by another substance while preserving the original structure. Common replacing agents are pyrite, hematite and silica."

I had a ready ear for your mother's humanistic sympathies. And I think it was clear to her from the start there were energies in our house circling out of family orbit. Mrs. Paige off to Wednesday night Bridge with a Mr. Raditz, who suffered her poor card memory for the other rewards of her company. Too, there were Mrs. Paige's Sunday excursions with her sister Elaine and the occasional gentleman Elaine had snared during the week for a consort. I invited your mother into a conspiracy of my own discontent. Meanwhile you looked at me with baleful suspicion, and passed your doubts to Martin.

I think it's fair to say you were already aware of yourself sexually, that you enjoyed and were mystified by yourself as an emerging woman. In fact your ingenuous modesty amused all of us. I remember my impatient wife knocking on the bathroom door, and you, panicky, calling out, "Wait a minute!" Then "All right!" after hastily covering your lack-of-bosom with a tee shirt, leaving your bottom half fully exposed.

It might disturb you to know that I just interrupted this recollection to study a color photograph of you and your mother posed on our sofa, both of you mugging for Mrs. Paige's camera. Your hair, cloned from Dolores's, mingles with hers as if the two of you were joined at the scalp by red flame. The two of you competing for the camera's eye are merged into one.

At pretrial my lawyer argued: Nothing so untoward could have happened in such a closely regulated, such a fully scheduled household. Of course this was ridiculous, but no more outlandish than the way your man pounced on the weakness:

"Scheduled! Exactly! Look at the routine. Isn't it a fact that while Mrs. Paige was at Wednesday night Bridge, the mother was obliged to be at weekly teach-

ers' meetings at her school, leaving the accused alone in
the house with her children?"

Yes, both women were gone on Wednesday
evenings, the time in the week you and Martin chose
for major rumpus, until I tamed the two of you with
some of my secrets. I let you look inside my great
uncle's tool chest. You and Martin pulled out every tool
and put every one back in its place, charmed I think by
the order of it and the idea that these simple instru-
ments, none of them with an electric cord, had built
your house. Then there were the marbles—the collection from my own childhood, agates, cats' eyes, and the
big shooters with milky swirls—which I allowed you to
win from me in games on the living room rug.

I know your mother blames herself for helping to
ease your suspicion of me. She couldn't help but take a
side in the running battle between us Paiges. My wife
was so public in her disenchantment with me. Her dissatisfaction with our house made this inevitable.

Didn't Delores agree, she asked, that I walked too
heavily, disrupting the peace in a room that had creaky
floors to begin with? Could she see that I chewed my
food with unbearable ostentation, that my mumbling
disgust with a newspaper was beyond endurance, that I
loaded the dishwasher incorrectly, that our living room
was cold. It was a state of mind; the list of particulars
had no end.

My career was an embarrassment to her: "He could
have used his education. Even if it was only to teach

children how to parse a sentence. But no, he had to work for the railroad." She told this to your mother whose own husband had worked for the B&O, and not on the office side, but in the yards. To Dolores, who had the integrated knowledge of a dedicated teacher, and could appreciate the thrill of a continental network of steel, an ear to the rail, a gigantic momentum approaching.

What *about* the Wednesday evenings? Your mother's rule that you should not come up from your basement room was repeatedly broken. First by your mischievous and rude adventuring—did you teach your brother to say "old prick," or did he pick it up in the school yard?—later by the allure of the marbles. Your resistance crumbled when you saw that I'd lose them with good grace.

Impatient to win them all, you even dared the door of my bedroom to study the glass mysteries of the last few in my bureau. Maybe you stole a few; I wasn't sure. When they were all yours we began the Wednesday evening story hours; you and Martin beside me on the bed as I read from the *Jungle Book*, in full trust at last, nuzzling close as you might to a father, as if you feared the drawings of mongoose and cobra might spring from the page.

On several occasions Martin fell asleep and was carried down to his own bed in my arms. Perhaps these evenings of release from your basement prison have been tainted by the shame of their secrecy from the absent jailor, your mother. But soon enough Dolores was aware of the bedtime reading. The game was up when Martin woke with a jungle nightmare, and asked her to check under his bed for snakes.

No, nothing untoward on Wednesdays. But what about Sundays, when Mrs. Paige went gallivanting with her sister, and your Uncle Davie came by to take you and Martin on his "urban adventures"? Zoo, museums, the amusement park. He was too flashy for your mother's taste, but he was eager to serve as leading male influence on his dead brother's children. He bought you too much candy, and, childless himself, was slow to learn that the way to a young heart is not a direct or pushy path.

Alone, your mother and I were free to attend what we called our Sunday services. Unbelievable? It was a sect of our own invention, half serious, the Church of the Fossil Record. A congregation of two, meeting at the kitchen table after noon, when Dolores had finished with her grading and lesson plans for the week ahead.

Our new faith was codified on paper napkins. I named it, Dolores wrote the founding credo: "We give science its way with creation back to time's first tick, knowing the mystery of the Watchmaker will abide forever."

I saved all the napkins, and I'm attaching one of them to this letter. That's your mother's handwriting isn't it? I don't think you'll deny it.

At her school they were at pains to make a science of their belief that the earth was brought forth from a word one happy day a few thousand years ago. Your mother's answer was sainthood for Copernicus, Keppler, Newton, Darwin, Einstein, Bohr, Feynman, and more to follow as their contributions were affirmed or refined. And each sedimentary layer with its fossil honored as another page of our revolving bible, the earth, millions of years in the writing, only one copy in circulation.

We were two happy initiates, spinning corollaries from our first beliefs. For example, as children of the same century and planet, didn't we have duties of love beyond national boundary and family border? We were looking for each other's affection. That's all.

And our answer was, "Of course." Would your family be here in our house otherwise?

Things better left unsaid. Besotted with the childish generosity of our new faith, I rushed to affirm her new beatitude. Blessed are they who walk beyond convention. I was an admiring disciple, and fully aware that our code was also an excuse for intrigue, a danger to our combined household.

One Sunday, sitting at our meeting, Dolores gave me a fishy look, and after a long silence asked, "Do you think you're finished?" I knew well enough what she meant. Would I remain there for the duration, a pigeon for my wife's target practice? Or would I take a chance with the rest of my life. "Just watch me," I said.

By April your house was under roof. The finish carpenters were almost done when the production company came from New York to make the testimonial minute for the insurance underwriters. Collins Ford went to its knees with the servility of a conquered population. Adults connived to be extras, children asked for autographs of the long-haired commercial auteurs with clipboards and jeweled watches. The same ones who trampled a lawn, closed the street without permit, and lounged in the coffee shop like Hollywood generals.

After all, your family and I were the real players. You were so proud: "We're going to be on television," you said, "because our house is fixed and we didn't pay anything for it." Asbestos was put around the windows, a smoke machine was installed, and large gas jets. "Nothing will burn," you promised Martin, "but there'll be fire engines. And Mr. Paige is coming for you again with his ladder."

The filmmakers left for a few days to prepare another job, promising to return the next weekend for a Saturday night shoot. Do you recall how excited you were that week, flapping around my house like the last of the whooping cranes? How many times did you throw your arms around my neck for a reassuring hug and my pledge that when the time came I would not let Martin fall? All of this turned now to my vile overture.

It rained that Saturday, right through the evening. Production was postponed to the following night.

There was a fuss among the film crew that showed their actual contempt for the project. Would they receive time and a half or double time? Sunday afternoon you didn't want to leave with Uncle Davie for fear he'd bring you home late. Dolores made you go, and then sat with me in the kitchen for our last service before the return to your own house.

There was only going to be a lawn between us again, but your mother and I stared at each other like parents of a tragic family about to be separated by a war or an ocean. Did I think, she asked, that the coming night would be a ceremony of lost innocence?

For us? Her children? Or did she mean the selling of our privacy? I dared not ask for fear of an awkward presumption that would ruin the moment. Wherever we were tending there was no push or pull, though I believe that after our fingers joined across the table and we were finally standing hand in hand, she bent toward the basement room, while I gave the winning nudge in the direction of the stairway to my own bedroom.

A seduction? Nothing so calculated. If our romance were graphed, the bed made up in Mrs. Paige's favored blue linen was the point where the steep curve of our affection met the more gradual slope of courage. I wouldn't have remembered that but again, your mother wrote it down, and I saved it. She also wrote that vice and shame were off plotting themselves in an ignored negative quadrant. Should we blame her for these strained conceits? After all, she was trained as a math instructor, and then asked to teach dogmatic religion.

If it's caddish to divulge so much about your mother, what choice have you left me? As it happened, we lay there under the covers discussing our predicament, paralyzed for a time by the prospect of complete intimacy. Our cerebral devotion had jumped ahead of its intention. I don't deny the consummation. What else after so long a naked embrace? Our heads were drowsy in the pillows when Martin's face appeared in the doorway.

"I don't want your help coming down the ladder," he said.

With calculated impertinence the two of you had tricked your Uncle Davie into bringing you home early. You went immediately to the basement to dress for your acting debut—the director only expected a nightgown—while Martin came straight to my room to announce his performance would be free of my helping arms. What he saw—your mother and me in the blue bedclothes—must have been unbelievable or inconvenient to the appropriate excitement of the evening.

The crew had everyone dressed and at their marks by nightfall. The smoke machine sent a white cloud from your new bedroom window. A man was telling your mother her hair would have to come down.

"Gorgeous," he said, but by then he meant the flames shooting out of the house. They wanted a more casual drape to your mother's bathrobe, a less severe knot in the sash. An hour later they were still not satisfied with her reaction sequence. When they found she wasn't good at tears they blew some real smoke in her eyes.

You and Martin were exhausted with all the retakes. A neighbor in the crowd, someone not chosen as an extra, called to your mother: "I see you finally taught Martin how to make an eternal flame." Fire kept coming out of your windows, but nothing was destroyed. With your home still a charade of smoke and flame at midnight, Martin was sobbing. "I never meant to start it," he told Delores, who wept, at last, for him, on camera.

"A wrap," someone consoled her.

"No," she said, "I'm warm."

The script girl chuckled into her palm.

We carried Martin to his bed, hoping the memory of what he'd seen that afternoon had been consumed in the artificial fire. Delores allowed me to tuck you in for the first night in your new room.

"This is *our* house," you said.

The Sunday meetings between your mother and me continued for a few months, always in my house. There was no more childish theology. Gradually we put intimacy aside. There was so much to discuss—the certainty of her dismissal at the Academy, though it never happened; your breathtaking advance to maturity, Martin's slow recovery from the night he had moved the candle too close to the window shade. I think Delores was pleased that I was really more interested in being a father than a husband. We were learning to be neighbors again.

The commercial appeared the next season surprising us with its thorough dishonesty, the polishing of motive to a sentimental fault, the false sequencing, the house bursting into flame and a cut to your mother's tears. We were shamed by our parts in the deception.

The legal maneuvering continues, and my house is still searched for damning evidence. The fools knock on the walls as if they were sheetrocked and hollow. They're even digging in the yard; what else did you tell them, Deirdre? How confounding is the search for history when the dust on an old skeleton is sifted and brushed by such earnest truth seekers?

You're offering an old man a way out the back door of a house he'll never leave: recant, resettle, take counseling in a distant city. All this you ask in the name of your mother, a founder of the Fossil-Record Church, who taught her most eager disciple to repeat after her—read it on the enclosed napkin—While the shape of the past endures, it may be filled with the counterfeit.

*You could see her luxuriating in
the attention, taking in warmth
at the pores.*

9

The Magellan House

In the early years the Mouras went to Santo Antônio do Porto only in June, when their vacation cottage could be kept a whole month for the price of a banker's dinner in Lisbon. It was a full morning's journey there in the aging Renault, with luggage strapped to the top and fishing rods through the windows.

The annual respite from the work year must have gone back beyond Polegar's clear memory to a time when he thought "damn it" meant get in the car and shut up, and his sister Christina's moments of affection were still cherished. Leaving the hot dust of the south for their perfect bay on the Atlantic Coast, he pitied the cork and eucalyptus trees rooted in place as the car rolled on, past castles and goatherds.

By the time he was nine and Christina sixteen, the vacation seemed more desirable than ever. The lower street and public square of the village would be covered with carnival rides, stalls, and attendant gypsies, and cabanas strung along the beach like endless rows of playhouses. But the trip that year was a trail of ill temper, with stops for threatened beatings. All, he believed, caused by his sister's nasty faces, her rearrangement of luggage in the back seat to her advantage, and little cruelties too subtle for the court of family justice.

Like other children, he called his parents Mãe and Pai; devotion and obedience built into the very sounds. So why should his name come from *pulga*, the flea, to *polegar*, the thumb and nail that squash it? Diminutive, pesty, it would never have been allowed by the censors in the Civil Registry where he was officially José Ricardo Moura. Too late. His schoolmates had hold of Polegar and would not let go.

What chance against Christina María Santa Veronica de Jésus, favored with a whole church calendar of suffering and adoration. Only a child like himself, he'd thought, but already in the long body of a woman who had arrived at knowledge she could not share. She called him Pulga for short, let her hair down in school against their mother's order, and lied in church.

"Father, I have nothing to confess, unless it is my pride in being able to say so." Polegar had sat in a pew next to her confessional thrilled by the chance she took with her soul. As if she'd not taken coins that week from Mãe's offering box. He hadn't reported her and might be trifling with his own salvation on her account. She was a caution to them all. Mãe had said so.

"Pai," Christina probed on the road, "the men you despise so much, don't they have names?"

"Christina!" Mãe's shrill warning from the front seat bought ten kilometers of silence. Pai spat out the window as they passed the army barracks, and then they were in the town called Baths of the Queen.

Here soldiers on short leave walked through the park with loaded pistols on the hip, the public security forces went by twos, and any man in an ill-fitting jacket was concealing a shoulder holster. And here they stopped each year to use the public toilets, and for Pai to go around the corner for the ritual gift—the cherry liqueur his wife took as her digestive after seafood. A sweet red syrup against the black ink of squid.

"Shall I open it now, Anna?"

"Not in front of the children, Paulo!"

She slapped Pai's naughty hand, and Christina groaned. As if she and Polegar didn't know the local brand of *ginja* came already decanted in a smooth ceramic phallus, upright, circumcised, and looking for all the world like anatomical Easter chocolate. In Santo Antônio it would be put on a high shelf, out of sight.

A half hour later they were in the crystalline microclimate of the village they loved. For Polegar, who had seen an aerial photo, Santo Antônio was a protractor like the one carried in his school kit since first grade, still unused. Its curve was a two-mile semicircle of white sand, and its straight edge, the line of cliffs over the Atlantic with a narrow cut in their center allowing the ocean in to touch the beach.

In the protected bay, so perfectly shaped and commodious it was called the Marquesa's Bidet, the surf was only a gentle lapping. Once a resort to royalty, Pai explained, now to the privileged, who looked down from their manor houses on the hillside over the quay, their holidays charmed by the fishermen and small merchants far below.

The Mouras' cottage was theirs by informal covenant, too old now to be broken. It had been servants' quarters to the grand old majolica-tiled house above it. Senhor Carvalho opened the small cottage only in June, suffering them into the playground of the wealthy, as it were, through a back door. His wife would appear in the cottage two or three times during the month to ask what was needed. Actually, according to Polegar's mother, to check on breakage.

The two Carvalho boys were not to be trusted at all, she said. Irreligious, private-school sneaks, each with his own little sailboat, one blue, one red. Polegar watched them dart back and forth on the bay as if it were the water of their own yacht club, narrowly avoiding the fishing boats. The older one, Pedro, Mãe accused of staring impertinently, and Maximino, she maintained, would not look her in the face. Polegar saw the contradiction; Christina dared to speak it. "What are they supposed to do with their eyes?"

That June the boys' younger sister, Inés, was the first Carvalho to greet them. Like Christina, sixteen. An appropriate friend, Mãe said, for her daughter, and the only Carvalho child she could really trust. Inés had once taken Christina into the big house, off limits to the rest of them. It has four baths, Christina had reported, and more. Inés had her own room with a little crystal chandelier and doors that opened onto a private balcony overlooking the bay. The dining-room table reflected silverware from the sideboard, and the room's white wood trim shone with the depth of enamel.

Passing on the sidewalk, his mother would touch one of the lovely tiles that covered the mansion from ground to eave, and moan as if pained afresh by its beauty. The way the blue design bled into white, each square a separate masterpiece. If Polegar slid his hand over them, it was just to wipe a little snot from his fingers.

The Magellan house, they called it, though how the Carvalho portraits on the paneled walls might connect the family with the great navigator had not been explained. Didn't every town on the Portuguese coast have a family who claimed to live in the Magellan house?

Even so, the Carvalho pretension was a comfort to the Mouras. It pleased them in their tight though adequate space to have something to snicker at. Polegar's father had tried to describe how thin a trace of Magellan blood anyone could claim after the meandering of twenty-five generations.

Polegar knew long before his mother that Inés was not to be trusted, that her church-scout uniform with its brown scarf and green jumper was a disguise for other activity. She bought magazines that had to be carried from the newsstand in brown wrapping, and went off to swim at forbidden beaches up the coast where Pai said the undertow could pull you all the way to America. Polegar could imagine Inés washing up on the hook Massachusetts stuck into the ocean, the place where his cousins lived.

Christina had resisted Mãe's push toward the daughter of the fancy house. Lucky for Christina. If she kept her distance from the rich girl, they could all return from vacation alive. But this year Polegar saw immediately it was going to be different. When Inés entered the cottage her eyes met Christina's with a knowing glance, and his sister asked to be excused from family plans so she might walk in the village with her friend.

"What's your father humming?" Inés was alert.

"His revolutionary anthem." Christina's honesty startled them all, and Inés, having discovered a pit, was not afraid to look for snakes. "What are the words?"

"Christina! What rubbish! There are no words, dear," Mãe assured the inquisitive girl.

Polegar remembered asking, "If there aren't any words, how can it be an anthem?" though he'd known there would only be trouble in that direction. With his sister gone he'd have to play on his mother's nerves until he, too, was released into the village. And though she slapped his face, he was sorry for provoking her. Polegar understood this was the place they came to escape his father's silent rage, where neither He Who nor the pope need be mentioned for a whole month.

He Who—short for he who dictates—was family code for the prime minister, also called "our economic genius" by Senhor Moura, who worked eleven months of the year as foreman in a ceramic block factory. He had chronic bronchitis, and made half the salary of an ordinary soldier in He Who's army, and a quarter the pay of one of his secret police. His bitterness had been struck into Polegar not with ranting but with a soft and repetitive tapping, as if a stonecutter had been working privately on a message for the ages. It said: This is what happened to me.

Twenty years earlier as a boy of eighteen, Polegar's father had been in the Rossio station in Lisbon, late at night, waiting with two friends for the train home to Torres Vedras. All in high spirits after a picture show. Another boy joined them, and at once they were arrested by He Who's police. A gathering of four after curfew was, on its face, a conspiracy. They were held overnight, questioned, and beaten for their attitudes. After that Polegar's father was on a list to be questioned at any time, hauled in without warrant. "Why would they need a paper from a judge? They arrest judges, too." The spite had to be squeezed through tight lips.

In Santo Antônio the anger could drain away with the tide. Here Pai went surf fishing with cronies from the market, grilled sardines with the construction workers in the lower town, and built a smile on the dark wine they poured from gallon jugs.

In Santo Antônio his father shed the year's defensive skin. He even brought his shortwave radio out of its box, and allowed Christina to tune in Radio Free Portugal after dark. Christina, who shook her long black hair to rock music via Morocco, refused to translate lyrics for Polegar. Or for her parents.

His sister was the only one of them with enough English to blush at the words. Between the songs were messages in Portuguese, seditious news that Mãe pretended not to hear and that Christina dismissed for impotence.

Polegar saw it was his sister who made the family different. Not only because her wide, round eyes and lithe figure could turn a head. It was her mind, which darted here and there, stunning her teachers, winning all the prizes in their school. Grabbing the answer to a math problem from the air before the pencils tapping around her touched paper. Spitting history's dates like so many grape seeds. And ready that season to bolt into political insolence. Pai was challenged to keep up.

In Santo Antônio they lived behind the shield of their landlord's wide influence. Though they despised the Carvalho fortune built on thousands of acres of grapevines and implicit homage to He Who, they could still relax in the good graces of power. For Christina to take up with Inés, Mãe seemed to believe, would be all to the good. For her daughter's political and Christian soul, an island of safe thought.

"Go ahead, and mind what Inés tells you," as if Inés would know better rules of decorum than Polegar's mother. So like his mother to be muttering "no better than we are" as she made the extra kettle of potato soup that Christina would be told to carry up to the big house—first gift in the month's little war of pleasantries. While Mãe cooked, she'd try to be angry at "the kind of waste going on up there," the quantity of beef and cod thrown into garbage cans.

She probably resented never being asked into the big house. She reproached the ease of wealth but longed for a look at the master bathroom where, according to Christina, the bidet, carved from a single piece of marble, had a frieze of angels below the rim, their eyes raised to the steamy world above. Mãe believed the way into the Magellan house, moated with formality, was over the bridge of Inés' friendship, and this June, Christina might at last oblige her.

Set free, Polegar followed the trail of the two girls down the steep cobbled walk, past the wide platform of the Super Troll, central attraction of the carnival, the bumper car ride. Each June his sister was "Super Troll" in the family. The name only meant the irresistible beggar she became each night without the fare to ride.

The concessions were closed for the afternoon, and he went to investigate a gathering of older men and women at the beach wall. A fishing boat was being hauled from the water by oxen, but no one paid attention. Ladies had their backs to the sand. He overheard "four Canadian women . . . the police have been called," and then someone reached out, trying to turn his head away from the bay. There, bobbing in the water with breasts uncovered, were the four from Canada, flouting the law of He Who's beaches. And sitting far out on the sand, chins on their knees, taking it all in, were Christina and Inés.

More than enough news to report back to the cottage if it had not been more important to keep his sister in sight. Two policemen had arrived. Watching through the cold lens of duty, they spoke only to each other, and moved off again. With that, the people's vigil lost virtue; they began to drift away. He hid in wait behind the wall until Christina and Inés began their walk home.

He knew precisely the distance he must keep. Far enough behind not to provoke Christina, and close enough to miss nothing she said, though she was mostly listening to Inés. "Where we go in France they all swim that way."

"The police did nothing."

"Of course not." Inés, bored with the obvious, nevertheless explained why the government did not want tourists bothered, and Polegar followed the two girls up the hill. Christina was being asked up to the big house again; he was shunted off on the cottage path. The news he was bringing home, reduced from shocking to ordinary, went dry, and "nowhere" was his answer to "Where have you been?"

At dark the carnival machinery began to turn, recorded music boomed up through the stone alleys, and thousands of lights blinked in the undulant motion of the rides they decorated. A time of wild need when deals could be struck with little effort. Pai came across with the coins. In return Christina pledged deeply, repeating after him, "To keep Polegar with me at all times. To treat him with honor as my own blood."

Her style on the Super Troll was all her own. She rode with a chin-up, how-dare-you face, as if the cars had not been designed for collision. Fingertips on the wheel and elbow resting on the frame, she imagined herself parading in a sports car too fine to be scratched. Polegar was used to waiting for the crash.

That night it was Pedro and Max Carvalho from the blind side, with Pedro, the older one, steering. Riding alone, Christina was no match for the momentum of their calculated impact. Her head snapped forward, and she was led off with a bloody lip. Bad fish to Pedro Carvalho.

The year before, hadn't he injured a swimmer, a village girl, with the centerboard of his sailboat? Pedro, one of the handsome boys from Oporto, too rich to be held to account! He seemed puzzled by Christina's accident. Too late with his apology. She was moving away through the crowd.

This time there was valid news to bring home. Something to put the vacation in order, and bring his sister back into the safety of the cottage. But again, he'd misjudged. His mother only moved for reconciliation. "You mustn't judge Inés by her brothers." His father was equally obtuse. "If I were a young man, wouldn't her car be just the one to aim at?"

Without asking, Christina took the shortwave set to her bedside and tuned in the bad signal. With her swollen lip and rage, she made a splendid martyr, turning the poisonous noise up to the world that abused them. So loud they might hear it through the windows of the Magellan house.

Mãe hurried to Christina's side with the glass of water she always placed on the playing radio.

"Not thirsty."

"Not for you, dear." She reached down to touch the swelling.

"I've told you that doesn't work," Pai called from the other room. "You might as well crawl all the way to Fatima."

Clear enough what was happening. His Pai and sister outdoing each other to prove their courage, while

Mãe prayed for their safety and maneuvered for the kind regard of the Carvalho family.

Let the water stay, Polegar pleaded silently, as if a glass of water might keep the wrong people from the door and save the vacation from disaster. From his bed across from Christina, noises off and lights out, he heard the good murmuring and the pouring of the *ginja* that would send his parents giggling off to their own kind of sleep.

The next morning Senhora Carvalho sent her housekeeper down with two blouses.

"She thought these would be nice for your Christina. How is her face?"

Castoffs of Inés, a little circle of grease on the collar of one, buttonhole torn on the other. From Pai a fist and forearm right up to the elbow for the condescension. Lucky the lady didn't see it.

Into the trash with the gifts? Not yet, because the poor woman also brought the summons so long wished for by his mother.

"Senhora says you will come for dinner tomorrow. All of you, yes?"

So much to do, Mãe complained. What flowers to take? Wine? Oh, I wouldn't know what kind! What dress to wear? What clothes to put on you children?

"Wine? He owns half the grapes in the Douro!" She was determined to make a fool of herself, Pai said. "Dress as we always dress and take nothing."

Over his mother's protest they showed up at the big house in their usual motley, and were immediately put at ease by geniality. All so smooth, the Carvalhos gallant to a fault inside the walls of their intimidating home. Pedro was scolding himself for a bully, insisting on Christina's pardon, leading her off to a grassy terrace. Max brought out cards, and sat down to play with Polegar as if really pleased to be matching wits with a provincial child, and Mr. Carvalho put a drink in Pai's hand, inviting opinion of the new gypsy camp, "Part of the cost of living in Europe?"

Polegar saw he could whip Max at the game if he chose. More important to catch everything his father said. The magnificent house might have gone unremarked in the sudden Carvalho graciousness, but the Senhora and Inés had moved quickly to oblige his mother's curiosity. They led her away, agape at the artful detail in the high plaster ceilings. And Senhor Carvalho had a little confidence for his father. "You know, *we* have a shortwave, *too*. One can't stop children from hearing other opinions. Some things will have to change, don't you think?"

"What I think wouldn't count for much." Polegar's father drank deeply and extended his glass in friendship. "My wife thinks if you put a glass of water on the radio, the security can't tell what signal you're listening to."

The two men chuckled.

"Where did she hear that?" Carvalho asked.

"On the Russian station. The one from Czechoslovakia."

"But why would the Russians put their friends at risk here? Why help our government?"

Cued for a favorite observation, his father couldn't stop himself. "Left, right, they mean nothing. One tyranny will always support another."

Senhor Carvalho was nodding and wondering aloud what good could come of the latest trouble at the local barracks. Pai's face went blank, as if his political stripe were not already clear on his sleeve. And Mãe came back to the cottage whispering it was true. Angels were circling inside the bidet.

One visit had turned the remote family into confidants. All following the lead of Senhor Carvalho, who seemed to have found an attractive mischief in his tenant. A dozen years of distance set aside with a few impetuous words. Now he was coming to the cottage to ask Pai up for the evening beer. "Bring the little boy with you. Maximino likes playing with him." It was easy for Polegar to rout the dull-witted Max at his silly card game, and a bore to be patronized by him.

Senhora Carvalho found new time for his mother, encouraged her to come by in the afternoons to walk on the meadows below the cliffs, and share the pleasures of an amateur botany. Where Mãe had been satisfied with the red glory of poppies waving on the hillside, she was now directed to manifold secrets under that gaudy carpet.

She came home with new veneration for her landlady and fragile petals to press between the pages—of what? No dictionary of flora in the cottage. No bookshelves. Only a magazine rack. And from her husband, a snort if a pale specimen fell into his lap as he leafed through an old number.

Worst for Polegar was the sudden loss of Christina to the team of Inés and Pedro. Perhaps they couldn't accept that his sister might be beyond reach of their wealth. They began to take her everywhere with them. Gave her lessons in how to be rich—how to hold a cup of espresso, a cigarette, the tiller of a sailboat.

Inés' cool, oval face was treated with softening lotions, and colors brushed about the eyes from a rainbow of little bottles. This was the ideal held up to Christina. Inés was moving from complete self-absorption to a preparation of his sister.

"Look at you, Christina, Pedro thinks you're wonderful, but your skin. So dry!" There were glances behind Christina's back, and whispering.

"Are you ready, Christy?" Inés at the door again, and Pedro, without license, at the wheel of one of his father's cars. "Have you brought the right bathing suit?"

Which meant they were on the way to the wrong beach, where the Canadian women had taken their sport. For the sin of it all, wouldn't the undertow drag someone out to sea?

Polegar couldn't follow, and no one else was home to save Christina. His mother walking with the woman who spoke Latin to weeds, Pai off with boozy fishermen, maybe boasting of his new sway with his landlord, whom he'd taught to say "He Who" with a sneer.

They'd been in Santo Antônio little more than a week, and now Polegar was leaving with Pai for the big house each evening after supper. There he'd sit crosslegged on a rug from India opposite Max, who said Polegar would do better if he'd stretch his memory. The men sat above them in deep leather chairs that seemed to absorb harmlessly all attacks on the state. More beer was poured.

"At least," Senhor Carvalho was grateful, "there's the Church for balance."

Pai raised a hand to demur. An institution always falling into the wrong hands, serving the wealth and vanity of the few.

No argument from his host. "All this time, Paulo! Who knew we had so much to share? And the children have finally discovered each other."

Later, Polegar could imagine the way Senhor Carvalho would have pulled his chin into a wise point as he gave the orders: Maximino, you'll take on the little one. Let him win on occasion. Pedro, Inés, I trust the two of you can gain the confidence of the proud daughter. (All this and more.) Your mother will distract the Senhora, and I'll handle Senhor Big Talk.

Polegar could not be everywhere at once, couldn't monitor his father's nightly bluster while trailing his sister through the carnival onto the beach, watching her mingle hands and glances with the rich boy turned gallant. Christina bought night freedom from Polegar with Super Troll fare, but small coins could not buy off infinite curiosity. He soon saw how the two ambled off through the shadows to find an empty cabana.

Inés must have known her work was nearly done. He heard her excuse herself. "Pedro needs time alone with you, Christina. I know! Take him into one of the tents. He's much too shy to ask you."

Shy? No trace of self-consciousness before this. In that family only Maximino suffered from self-aware-ness. His bluff and presumption, all imitation. "Another vapid day in paradise," presented as original malaise, would have been learned an hour earlier from his brother.

It had been Polegar's duty that summer to watch and listen in silence as his father and sister went leap-frogging over one another's nerve. At a discreet dis-tance from the chosen tent he learned that a persuasive lie—"It's all right, Christina. We aren't children"— might be followed by an odd, diminutive moaning, what he would call her squeaking noises when it came time to tell.

Fed up with nightly romance, he had gone again with Pai to the big house where the men had progressed to brandy and the folklore of failed assassinations. "A bazooka would have been easy." His father rising ardently from his chair, whistling his palm through the air in a slow arc. "The Thursday night poker game in the Brazilian Embassy. He Who used to come in the side door. Everyone knew about it."

Perhaps Inés understood that time was short. Returning to help her brother and Christina over another hurdle, she had brought her guitar to a tent tryst and plied them with *fados*. All the sad news of incomplete love in her soft, clear voice. Unwanted beach strays gathered to admire.

Another night Senhora Carvalho had pulled the grown-ups off to a play at the House of Culture in the nearby town. Dumped by the older children, Polegar wandered about the carnival, and came home to a cottage lit by one dim candle. Through the window he saw Christina, Pedro, and Inés sitting down to the kitchen table with the shocking decanter of *ginja* in front of them.

The three were watching one another, motionless, until Inés took her brother's hand, placed it on the clay shaft, and helped him pour for Christina. Nothing was said. And now Inés did the same with Christina's hand, gently guiding it to fill Pedro's cup. Like little gods and goddesses for whom ritual was serious symbol. Polegar reeled off into the sinning night. When he came home again the *ginja* had been put away, the cups were gone, and the house empty.

At a small hour, still awake on his bed, he listened to his parents prepare sentences of increasing severity for the absent Christina. House arrest, beating, a convent school, which they could not afford.

She came home conceding nothing, though she couldn't deny where she'd been. The smell in her clothes and hair was too heavy to escape Mãe's twitching nostrils. Lying in the rosemary thickets in the high meadows. "You expect us to believe you went alone?"

The household was hardly down to chastened sleep when men came for his father, agents of Mãe's worst daydreams, dressed like fishermen but carrying the feared laminations in fast-flip wallets.

"No rush, Senhor Moura. Our people are not cruel."

He was told to take his wife and children home to Torres Vedras, to wait there. "There'll be time enough to tell us all about the bazooka."

Pacing through the night, Pai promised revenge on the weasel Carvalho. There were some kind of good-byes to be said to the informing landlord, but he and his family had already escaped for their northern residence.

Polegar was carsick. What castle? Damn the Moors, damn the Romans, damn the Castilians! Did his mother expect him to think now of history and distant patriotisms? As if she were interested at that moment in the ancient, shifting tenancies of the walled city they were passing, as Pai drove on, contemptuous, spitting out his window to prove it, toward surrender.

Mãe was frantic, trying to divert herself from the certainty of her husband in a cell. "What did you tell him, Paulo?"

Deflected, she faced Christina in the back seat. His sister, her eyes black with loathing for the family's ignorance, swore her friend Pedro could know nothing of what Senhor Carvalho had done.

"I expect you've got plenty to tell the priest."

"Not a thing," Christina complained, her lip trembling. "There's never anything to tell him."

"What about your squeaking noises in the cabana?" Polegar offered helpfully. "And drinking from the penis."

The car stopped. Pai got out and opened Polegar's door. Taking him by the arm, he marched him off through a eucalyptus glade, far out of sight of the highway.

His parents came home to the bitterest month, in which tears and recrimination were not cathartic. The screaming, the slamming shut and throwing open of doors, no relief. Pai returned to work. What else? To run was to put all their lives at risk. Mãe wondered if they'd come for him at the house after dark, or take him from the job. After dark meant no address, no return.

Every day she intruded on Christina's toilet. Christina threw the whole roll of paper at her. Mãe would have been sniffing around for his sister's blood, which was late. Christina's jaw was set tight, as if her summer sport could have been ennobled by her own honest thrall.

Maybe the rest of his sister's body knew more than her stubborn heart. How desperately it must have been working to reject the germ. A spontaneous flow a month later held for Mãe the redemption of God's own blood. Or was she so weepy-smiley because with each passing day her husband was a step further from arrest?

Another scare for He Who at a northern barracks. At the café Pai sat the reborn Christina across from him, poured her wine, and sang in her face his revolutionary anthem, with words. Mãe beat at his chest, begging him to be still, while Christina raised her glass, saluting audacity. There was a new verse in which tyrants dined on offal, the only remains of their informers.

Christina wouldn't be outdone. She rose in her classroom to give rote on a national fairy tale, the only kind of history allowed. Her instructor waited for the story of a baker woman who pushed a Spanish soldier into her oven, shifting the tide of battle six hundred years ago. Instead Christina named a revolutionary a martyr, she said, shot only months earlier. Polegar heard how his sister had been pulled from the room by her ear.

Now he could only admire the timing of Christina's defiance, and the lesson of his father's excess: choose that year in the life of a nation when recklessness becomes heroic. The year when carnations are placed in rifle barrels and soldiers are charmed away from one authority into the sway of another.

In the spring a single general called about face, and forty years were repudiated in a moment. Men with debts of blood and deceit fled the borders. The Moura radio played news of redistribution, of informers going underground, or leaving Portugal in fear for their lives. Lifted on the democratic tide, Polegar's family prepared for another June in Santo Antônio.

This time they entered the cottage like thieves. He was sent through a window to unlock the front door for his family. The Carvalhos were gone, probably following their money to the banks of northern Europe.

For the Mouras it was a time of careless retribution. On the cottage stoop there was a daily grilling of sardines, with old summer friends coming up the hill to drink from a common jug and congratulate the family on their bold entry—though it was soon clear Pai would not be satisfied with this. Rent-free occupation of the small quarters was too paltry a revenge.

Mãe protested, but the next week Polegar was raised to the balcony of the big house, where he forced his way through the glass doors of a bedroom and felt his way down the grand stairway to let the family in. Valuables and smaller effects were gone, but all the large furniture remained.

Invading every room, they threw shutters and windows open to the sun, tossed themselves on the beds, flopped down on chairs and sofas. Like giddy travelers testing a new hotel for comfort before deciding to spend the night. "Christina, you take the girl's room. Polegar, you'll be at the end of the hall. Anna, what do you think of this bed?"

Mãe, about to live in the house she most coveted, was arguing against it, predicting a summary eviction. Pai swept aside the fears. "The rats have run. The country is ours."

They went back and forth between cottage and mansion for a week or so before daring a full night in the big house. Nothing was said against them. There was only encouragement from other revolutionary spirits in the lower town. And a few days later the occupation was complete.

His sister took it casually. A matter of course that they should be there. For several months she'd been receiving curious notes from Pedro, postmarked Belgium. And they continued to arrive once the Mouras reached Santo Antônio. She would read the family a line or two and keep the rest to herself.

"We hear you've moved into the big house for the month. Whatever my family has done to yours . . . "

From what little she revealed, Polegar supposed that this letter, like earlier ones and those that followed, gave his sister a double pleasure. They seemed to affirm that Pedro had been *her* fool, and they gave her something of the Carvalhos to tear and burn once flattery had been absorbed.

". . . I will use what influence I have with my father," Pedro wrote her. Was this a warning, Polegar wondered, of trouble if they continued in the house?

Whatever the letters held of teenage mush was her affair. "Affair, exactly." Mãe found tricky resonance scattered all through Christina's talk. "Burn before reading," she warned. Wasn't it proven beyond quibble that teenage mush was dangerous mush? No end to her suspicion. Why would the boy keep writing to a silent correspondent?

No more dancing off to the wrong beaches. The two-piece bathing suit was replaced by one that covered the shoulders and had a little apron attached that fell to Christina's knees. Under her breath she said if she felt like it she'd take the whole damn thing off. Despite this, Polegar believed his sister was grateful for new restrictions that season, even for chaperoned evenings. That she felt a duty to heal a shameful sexual scar.

——✦——

No longer just a summer victory, the estate was a prize to be held—though the neighbors would begin to notice how the gardens were running down, unattended, with bamboo and brambles crowding up against the terraces. No one believed Pai's boast, that the place was getting its just deserts. So that a common man could one day live here without shame. A common man like himself. He had found another job with modest pay at a block and tile company a short distance inland.

For Polegar the house was a troubling surfeit of rooms, where the arrangement of Carvalho furniture dictated the pattern of the new routine. Mãe found some pleasure in imitating the privilege that preceded her, though she was always behind in her new war on dust and mildew as she went from room to room. Never mind, no bed was moved, not a table shifted.

A novelty to sleep and eat there. Polegar didn't know that the next few years of their lives would be marked by a struggle against decay. The year they let the south-end bathroom go out of use. The summer the damp stain reached halfway down his bedroom wall. The season they began to find woodworm tailings along the baseboards in Christina's room.

These were uneasy years. Years of waiting for the Carvalhos. And they did come home to Portugal. At first by proxy. All the letters from Pedro, and then the girl's face in a sappy television drama from Lisbon. Christina spotted her and called the family to watch the credits confirm Inés Carvalho was Queen Leonor.

Mãe was satisfied there was nothing to admire. "They bought her the part."

Polegar knew the only rent his family paid for the Magellan house was drawn from the balance on a moral debt. The one incurred in the summer of Carvalho treachery. Law and a new class of judges were making long-term squatters difficult to dislodge. Still, his sister was the only one who, as the years passed, felt fully at home here. The one who would be able to tell others about the living-room ceiling.

"A plaster bas-relief with cherubs in the corners holding up a woven garland. The centerpiece is a rose and geranium bouquet." How could she know all that or feel free to tell the world? Polegar never let his eyes linger on the rich surfaces.

Step by step, he could feel the ousted family coming back to them. Senhor Carvalho was seen in the corridor of the regional courthouse in conversation with one of the property lawyers. After that, Mãe assumed every stranger at the door carried eviction papers.

Pedro had written another letter to Christina. "Whatever damage our families have done one another . . . ," one of the soft messages that kept coming. His improbable postal suit. Love notes on legal paper?

Neither would the sister fade away. Inés' face insinuating itself over and over on their television. The glamor press had caught up with her racy biography. Nineteen now, and already a failed marriage, an alleged pregnancy, intimacy with another actress (photographed). From moral high ground they followed her career. Now she was Claudia, antiheroine of a telenovela. The one with the wide mouth painted wider, who had tried to electrocute her man, dropping a lamp in his bathtub. Inés had achieved the gaudy celebrity for which her childhood was rehearsal. A seamless transition to a profession of the way she'd always behaved.

In the magazines and tabloids she was drawn more tragically. Inés, grape heiress manqué. Daughter of the former wine baron with the highest political connection. His vineyards lost during voluntary exile after the revolution, the land doled out.

Actually, not so tragic for the Carvalhos, since the whole family was repatriated and doing well again. Even feckless Maximino, who had joined his father in hot coastal development. Senhor Carvalho worked the city in a silk suit, while Max was sent back to Santo Antônio in the baggy flannel of the common man, where his slow mouth, mistaken for innocence, best served the family interest. His job, to promise apartments in beachfront condominiums to those who'd commit their land to the future.

In Santo Antônio he'd found dozens of ways to avoid Polegar. Simple moves like turning his back, crossing to an opposite sidewalk, hiding his face in a newspaper, ducking into a café. Even the fictitious loss of a coin in the pasteleria, drawing his eyes to the floor.

Pedro was more a mystery. Polegar could only think of him as the shadow that crossed his sister's face when the boy's name was mentioned. Or as the postmark on his letters. And soon enough Pedro's postmark was Portuguese.

Christina had become secretary for the exhibition hall at the House of Culture, and bookkeeper to the ballet instructor there. She was bringing young men home to see the house—dancers and painters who struck poses with dangling cigarettes. They held her hand and looked over the bay from the overgrown terrace. They were artists of the fading revolution with their local heroine, the woman who, several years ago, had defied He Who, and claimed the mansion of an informer.

She was making Mãe pay for all that nervous attention to her dress and hygiene, going through her men much too quickly and without real interest. Obvious to Polegar. She encouraged him to come along if they tried to steer her further from the house. These men were not lovers, he was sure, but props brought around to show that an appropriate social need was being met.

"You ought to be getting on with your life," was Mãe's consent to some new passion for Christina. As long as it led to a church. Instead Christina had settled into a habit of privacy. Setting off to work, she showed the hard edge of a woman whose course is set. Wore clothes that straightened her figure, and heels that beat a staccato on the village cobble, warning strangers away.

On market days she went alone to Baths of the Queen, sailing out under false colors, as it happened.

Got up in the common black of bereavement offset by a white lace collar that might have signified her late commitment to chastity. And carrying a basket that came home filled with chard and kale, salt cod and turnip greens. As if her only rendezvous in the town had been with merchants, procuring the stuff of a bitter, healthy regimen.

"You could do something with your hair." If Mãe began that way, it could quickly turn bitter and confusing. "There's nothing wrong with you. Hold your head up. Listen to me. And don't play the saint around here."

If Mãe kept on, Pai might give her a sharp tap on the head and remind them all. "We're here. It's settled." Those people would be coming back over his dead body—though they'd already invaded the house countless times by mail and television. And a magazine with a photo of the whole Carvalho family gathered in honor of Inés' second wedding carried up to Christina's room. To laugh at? Stick pins in?

It was still easier for Polegar's father to scoff than relax in the spacious house. "What part Magellan could the people be if the great man himself went to Spain and married a Spanish lady?"

A friend of Christina from work had come visiting. A man who'd been the village soccer hero. Letting go of his athletic body gracefully, he spent his free hours at a chessboard brooding over the greedy direction the revolution had taken. He appeared with a rose, and recited for Christina from the Czech novel of the season. "But socialism should concede nothing to tyranny."

Maybe, maybe not. But what did this have to do with putting the flower in Christina's hair and kissing her neck? This was a man favored by Polegar's mother, one expected to do the right thing, come to Pai with a confession of his suit and prospects. A local man working on an honest political conscience, on views he must have supposed Christina would admire. She turned him away at the door.

"I don't have time," she said softly, inventing an excuse for this night and one for the next.

"What do you have time for?" Mãe hovering over another lost evening.

Television. They all had time for television. It's the hour of the telenovela, when they allow Inés into her old living room as electric, colored dots. A smear of red across the mouth, a bronze neck covered with rhinestones, and body wrapped in a tight, blue, silky tube, all moving to a theme of dissatisfaction.

Mãe sits alert, ready to be insulted all over again by Inés' character. And Inés gives her yet another moral victory.

"The part was made for her."

"She made herself for the part."

His mother and sister had even found a way to contest their full agreement.

"The wig is just right for her."

"She makes the wig look right."

The voices took on that edge again, when civility, as a sighing effort, became a provocation.

"Christina, why must everything I say be a target? Am I such a trial to you? Put on something nice, and let your brother take you for a walk."

"Something nice?"

She must have been waiting for that. She ran up to her room and came down moments later to strut in front of them, twirling the two halves of the banished bikini. Mãe dismissed the bathing suit with wistful satisfaction. "She doesn't have the shape for it anymore. She wouldn't wear it."

Polegar had imagined Senhor Carvalho living in fear of Pai. Why else had the challenge never come? For how long had they eaten, slept, and moved their bowels here before the first agent of the Carvalhos came to the door?

And what was there to show off to him but mildew in the front hall and their new ages? His complexion was already clearing. And Christina, grown up, with people beginning to ask Mãe if something were wrong with her daughter, still single.

Very apologetic, the man had been instructed not to disturb Senhora Moura. "There is a picture of Senhora Carvalho's mother when she was a child." He hesitated. "Needed for the coffin." He knew exactly where they should look. "The tall bureau in the second guest bedroom upstairs. Senhora says the drawer will stick this time of year."

"I'll have to ask my husband."

Mãe's hand trembled as she pushed the man back from the doorway. They'd all been warned. Any Carvalho entry, any concession, might have a disastrous consequence.

The next morning Polegar followed Maximino into the pastry shop, and caught him between the counter and another patron. "We're sorry about your grandmother," he'd expected to say, "of course your mother is welcome to the picture." But he was suddenly wary of healing. And his first words to Max were a false ignorance. "So whatever became of your sister?"

Max, sucking on his teeth, decided. "She's done all right." And he slid past Polegar with his own arch question. "Which room are *you* using?"

Instead of shouting at his retreat, "Your room, you prick!" Polegar let the moment evaporate and condense slowly into lost opportunity and regret.

Christina's new wardrobe that spring was not really daring according to the line coming north from Lisbon and gradually moving up the provincial leg. Mãe, being careful not to shame her, still coaxed without specificity. "Why don't you bring one of your nice men around?"

It didn't work that way with Christina. If you walked along the beach on a Saturday, you would see her out on the sand in the bikini, alone, reading Pessoa perhaps, or the fiction of some martyr of the Eastern bloc. The bathing suit no longer a provocation, even in the family. It was the common thing now for women from the cities and tourists to swim topless in Santo Antônio.

Walking out to call her home for lunch, Polegar was shocked to see Pedro Carvalho leaning against the beach wall, turned out in summer whites. And perfectly composed, as if he'd been dropped in from the Riviera to show how this scene could be played with style. No display of silver against a bare chest. Only sunglasses hanging under the one free button of his starched shirt. He stood absolutely still, studying the small area where Christina lay facedown in the sand.

It was apparent she knew she was being observed from the wall. No shrinking into her core of self-contentment. You could see her luxuriating in the attention, taking in warmth at the pores. Wriggling her frontal shape into the loving sand. Her legs bent back at the knee, feet waving a slow semaphore of satisfaction with Pedro's gaze.

Pedro strolled onto the beach and sat beside her. Without looking up, Christina reached out to touch his leg. They hadn't spoken, but now she rolled over to face him, and he leaned to kiss her forehead. Flat on her back, she was poking a finger into the soft, olive skin below her navel, pointing straight down. Reverently, Pedro placed his hand there.

When Polegar turned to leave they were still fixed in that same position of silent worship. He was agape with detail learned from mime alone, the devotion in the soft touch of lips to her brow. Their intimacy as public as the air they breathed. And clear to Polegar, even without the first hint of a swelling, there was going to be a child. That some faint fraction of a Magellan was already waiting in embryo under Pedro's hand.

He hurried up the path, more exhilarated than dismayed. Preparing himself for his parents, projecting into the future: There's a child in my sister's womb waiting a turn to bathe in the Marquesa's Bidet, and make a claim on a birthright home.

He slowed, catching his breath, considering the long deception of Christina's separate peace. But where was the fault in a deception so long anticipated by Mãe's nagging question, Why would the boy keep writing to a silent correspondent? He was like a child again, hurrying home to tell a tale on a slippery sister. This time with news that could not go dry in his mouth.

Christina confessed her story in pieces. That afternoon she admitted reacquaintance with Pedro, a season of market-day encounters. By suppertime she told how the two of them had been married a month earlier at the Civil Registry. Not planning to move in together until Pedro found the perfect house. Secrecy had only been meant to save the families from an awkward ceremony.

Perfect house? They knew it wasn't a house she needed. All she needed was for the rest of them to move out of this one. For Pai and Mãe to return to Torres Vedras, where they could at last feel at home again.

But why wouldn't a girl so radiantly happy proclaim her pregnancy to the world? She was in no hurry to drive them away. Perhaps Christina didn't announce her condition until she no longer felt comfortable in the bikini; far enough along that the sequence of marriage and conception, whatever it had been, was blurred by joy and the passage of time.

Mãe made another little show of indignation, though her patience had been winding down to "long enough." Pai had his own way of taming the news. "Haven't I explained it to you? After twenty-five generations we're all related to Magellans."

Within the week they were ready. The departure was dignified. Without tears. He followed his mother and father through the door. Outside, his hand slid along the lovely blue wall with a reverence due the home of kin. And Christina waved down to them from her balcony with all the confidence of a clever, fertile queen.

Acknowledgments

With thanks to Sarah McNally, Megan Hustad,
Emily Forland, Rich Lane, Maggie Siner,
and Phil Ehrenkranz.